The Thrice Named I

Part I

Scythian

The Thrice Named Man

Part I

Scythian

by

Hector Miller

www.HectorMillerBooks.com

The Thrice Named Man
Part I
Scythian

All characters and events in this publication, other than those clearly in the public domain, are fictitious and any resemblance to real persons, living or dead, is purely coincidental.

Author: Hector Miller

Proofreading: Kira Miller, J van Rensburg

First edition, 2018, Hector Miller

Part 1 in the book series The Thrice Named Man

ISBN: 9781718011625

Text copyright © 2018 CJ Muller

All rights reserved.

No part of this publication may be reproduced, stored in a retrieval system, or transmitted, in any form or by any means, without the prior permission in writing of the author. Publications are exempt in the case of brief quotations in critical reviews or articles.

Contents

Chapter 1 – Night after the harvest 1

Chapter 2 – Road to Sirmium 9

Chapter 3 – Procurator 13

Chapter 4 – Ride to Viminacium 21

Chapter 5 – Crossing the limes 25

Chapter 6 – Barbaricum 28

Chapter 7 – Confession 34

Chapter 8 – The story continues 49

Chapter 9 – Men of metal 53

Chapter 10 – Camp 57

Chapter 11 – Training 60

Chapter 12 – Warrior 67

Chapter 13 – Migration 71

Chapter 14 – Traveller 76

Chapter 15 – Recovery 83

Chapter 16 – The Huns 85

Chapter 17 – Leaving camp 95

Chapter 18 – Rude awakening 101

Chapter 19 – Rescue 111

Chapter 20 – Pursuit 120

Contents (continued)

Chapter 21 – Meeting 126

Chapter 22 – Life goes on 133

Chapter 23 – Time to leave 141

Chapter 24 – Going home 145

Chapter 25 – Arrival of the man 152

Chapter 26 – Back with the Roxolani 160

Chapter 27 – It starts 165

Chapter 28 – Meeting the Goths 175

Chapter 29 – Betrayal 194

Chapter 30 – Decision of the king 199

Chapter 31 – Hunting with Bradakos 208

Chapter 32 – Plan 217

Chapter 33 – Day of reckoning 223

Chapter 34 – Aftermath 230

Chapter 35 – Feast 235

Chapter 36 – Goodbye Bradakos 240

Chapter 37 – Crossing the Danube 244

Chapter 38 – Sirmium 248

Chapter 39 – Tribune 259

Chapter 40 – Decision 266

Prologue

For a thousand years, Rome had endured.

From the time of the kings, through the centuries of the Republic, Rome prospered. Great men such as Julius Caesar, Augustus and Trajan expanded Rome's dominion.

But a shadow is descending over the Empire. Hostile barbarian hordes are breaching the vast frontiers. Civil war, the plague and economic hardship are eating away at the very soul of Rome.

But the gods have not yet abandoned Rome.

From a humble background in Illyria, a boy emerges as the only hope of civilisation.

He is destined to accomplish the impossible.

This is the story of his journey.

Chapter 1 – Night after the harvest

Nik slowly rose to a standing position and placed a calloused hand in the small of his back. With pursed lips he regarded the golden fields that had turned to silver.

He smiled grimly, stretched, and pointed at the sky. "That's what they call a harvest moon, boy", he said. "There will be no rest until all is gathered." He turned his gaze to the east where ominous clouds were gathering on the horizon. "It will rain tomorrow, mark my words. We have to finish. If the wheat gets water, the black rot will claim it all."

I knew the worth of a sharp sickle. It made the backbreaking work bearable. But in the dim blue light of the moon, I cut my fingers and my hands. Deep, throbbing cuts.

The gods favoured us, and soon the last sheaves were under roof. Slowly we made our way to our room. Overcome by fatigue, we collapsed onto our beds, neglecting to give thanks to the gods and conveniently choosing to ignore the hunger.

I guess it was the combination of pain and exhaustion that kept me awake, or maybe the fact that Nik had promised me that we could go riding the next day. I heard soft whinnies emanating from the stables. Only a thin wooden wall separated the small room from the horses. It was Nik's room, but he allowed me to share it with him.

Nik was the oldest person I knew. I wasn't sure how old, but Nik told me stories about Marcus Aurelius and Commodus. Stories so convincing, I was sure he had known those great men. Just maybe Nik was a liar after all, but he was the only one who wanted me after Mother had died. So I forgave Nik, just in case.

Then I heard it - a sound I knew well. The sound of an arrow leaving a bowstring.

The horses stirred, but Nik continued snoring, oblivious to the happenings.

I rose from my straw mattress with the nimble movement only afforded to the very young, and retrieved my most prized possession from underneath the bed. My hand tightened around the hilt of my wooden sword that Nik had fashioned - the familiar feel of the smooth-worn pommel comforting me. Nik was teaching me. The old man said that he owed it to the gods. I didn't understand how one could owe the gods something. How things change.

The moon still bathed the yard in its waning light, allowing me to notice movement in the shadows.

Nik was a kind man, although there were rules. I was forbidden to wake him. Not that it mattered, because he was always the one who woke me. I was sure that I could break this rule once, maybe.

I shuffled across the rough stone floor and came to a halt beside Nik's bed, unsure of how to wake him. I had never done it before. Maybe the old man would get a fright and die. Maybe that was the reason why it was not allowed. Suddenly I doubted whether I should do it.

The horses whinnied again.

Panicking, I reached down and touched Nik's shoulder. In a blur of movement, I was on my back with the edge of a dagger pressed firmly against my neck. This didn't scare me, though. It was the look in his eyes that unsettled me. A look I had never seen before, cold and merciless. The menace disappeared as recognition dawned in the old man's eyes. He snapped away the dagger and hugged me close, his hands examining me for wounds.

"Lucius, are you hurt? Did I hurt you?" the old man whispered in panic.

I shook my head and hugged him. "Nik, there are men outside. I'm sorry I woke you", I stammered too loudly.

Nik placed a finger to his lips. He strapped on his sword and took his bow from the wall. And what a bow it was. I spent countless hours admiring the weapon. Nik once told me how it is made. Only a few men in the world possessed the skill. None lived within the borders of civilisation. These barbarian craftsmen use the finest of timber, dried for years. The wood is strengthened with many layers of deer tendons, meticulously glued and then covered in birch bark. The inside of the bow is plated with pieces of horn from a rare species of cattle, and fused together with glue derived from the intestines of a fish that lives far to the east.

The bow was a thing of beauty, yet it was as deadly as it was beautiful. Wielded with skill, it was more powerful than could be imagined. I knew, I had witnessed its power.

"Lucius, there are bad men outside. I will chase them away. Stay inside", Nik whispered as he took five arrows from his quiver. He did not wait for an answer, but there was enough authority in his voice to persuade me to obey.

Nik did not say I wasn't allowed to watch, though. I had enough common sense to not go to the window, and pressed my face against the wall where two planks were badly joined. The crack was wide enough to afford a good view of the yard. I vaguely recalled Nik mentioning the carpenter being executed due to poor workmanship. The old man repeatedly threatened to fix it, but during the harvest, time was at a premium.

Nik kept to the shadows of the outbuildings. Three dark figures approached the stables. They moved liked thieves - not the confident strides of men who belong. One man carried a bow with a nocked arrow while the other two had swords in their hands. They were about as far away as a boy could throw a good stone when Nik released his first arrow. The bowman crumpled with a shaft protruding from his head. Few archers used the technique of the Scythians where the arrows are held in the draw hand. The old man did.

The other two men died before the bowman had hit the ground.

Flames and smoke erupted from the main house, illuminating the three dead men and drawing the attention of the remaining four raiders. They advanced cautiously, but were silhouetted against the backdrop of fire. I heard the rapid twang of two arrows released in succession, and two more men lost their lives. One of the remaining attackers pointed in Nik's direction and approached his shadowy hiding place.

Nik had spent all his arrows. He relinquished his bow and stepped into the light.

The two men approached Nik from different directions. They were big, muscular men with close-cropped black hair and clean-shaven faces. Judging by the quality of their tunics and thickly woven red cloaks, they were no brigands.

"You know why we are here, old man. You knew we would find you eventually", the obvious leader hissed in unaccented Latin. "No man can hide from him, not even you. He wants your head, and the letter", he continued.

Nik remained silent and calmly strode to within sword range, facing the leader with his back to the henchman. He walked with the gait of an old man, with a slight limp. His gladius was sheathed, his open palms extended at his sides.

It was clear that Nik required assistance and I wished to lend a hand. Sometimes the gods intervene. If I had stepped outside that night, I would surely have been killed. What match is a boy for trained killers?

"Time to die, old man", the leader hissed, and grinned. He menacingly stepped closer to Nik and raised his long cavalry sword above his right shoulder, ready to strike. He wore the look of a man about to kill a lame, troublesome dog.

But with a speed and agility that belied his age, Nik stepped into the blow, drew his razor-sharp Gallic gladius, and with an upward strike severed the leader's hand at the wrist. The man fell, screaming, desperately clutching his arm, trying to stem the flow of blood. Nik put him out of his misery.

The second man's attack was lightning fast. He feigned to the right. Nik took the bait and lost his footing, going down on one knee. The man grinned and moved in for the easy kill. It was a manoeuver the old man had practised countless times. He blocked the strike using the power of his legs to propel himself upward, unbalancing his opponent. The henchman staggered backwards. Nik pivoted on his right heel and took the head with a single blow.

An eerie silence descended upon the yard. Nik returned to looking like an old man again. There was no sign of the skilled warrior.

I ran outside.

"Wine, boy. Bring me wine, the good stuff", Nik growled.

I ran back inside, filled his large wooden beaker to the brim and handed it to him as he entered the room.

"You take the first swallow, Lucius", he commanded.

I swallowed a huge mouthful of the dark red wine and handed it back to Nik, who finished it in one go and held the empty beaker for a refill. He sat down awkwardly on the edge of the bed and sighed, "That's better."

"Who were they, and what did they want with you?" I blurted out.

"It is a long, long story, my boy. I guess I need to tell you, eh? But before I do, we need to do a few things. Now go get my bow, I left it outside and I told you it might rain."

Chapter 2 – Road to Sirmium

The happenings of the previous evening had left me exhausted and I woke a full watch past sunrise. My eyes searched the room, but Nik had left without waking me.

My first thought was that it had all been a bad dream. I became aware of the acrid smell of burnt timber, and realised that the memories were real. Too real.

I found Nik at work at the charred remains of the villa. He was unceremoniously dragging the last of the dead attackers by the feet into one of the small freestanding store rooms. "Lucius, fetch an amphora of oil from the barn", Nik commanded.

I was clear that the old man was in a dark mood so I didn't consider voicing any of the questions that were milling around in my head. The answers would come in time.

I helped Nik to pour oil over the bodies. When we were done, he used a glowing ember from the smouldering villa to set the building alight.

As smoke poured from the window openings, Nik visibly relaxed. "Well, at least that is done", he mumbled.

He didn't look at me, but kept staring into the flames, emotionless. "Lucius. All the people who lived here are dead. Dead. All murdered by the men I had killed. Your friend

Plotius, old Rufius, even Gaius. All dead. The owner of the small estate Quintus Domitius, killed in cold blood. All the bodies of our friends burned with the villa and the labourers' quarters. There is nothing to say goodbye to. No one to bury. No mouths to place a coin into, no prayers to be said."

"Walk with me, boy", Nik growled as he turned around and slowly limped back to our room. "Lucius, now is the time for action, we will mourn our friends later. If this incident is not handled correctly, there will be questions. I will end up on a cross and you at the slave market. Let's see what we need to pack and get to Sirmium before the sun sets."

Fortunately the horses were all still safe. The carts, which were kept in the main barn, were however reduced to ash. It left us with no option but to travel light.

"I know Sirmium is only two-thirds of a watch away, Lucius, but I do not think that we will come back here. Pack what you need. Only what you need. And say your goodbyes. Do it with haste."

Nik and I saddled our favourite horses and chose two as spares. In addition, we each took a packhorse.

"We will take the weapons, the cooking pot, plates and mugs", Nik said. "I will buy a tent in Sirmium. Don't be concerned about food and clothes, we will buy that as well, but make sure you pack the red wine. Only the good stuff, though, the sour shit I can get anywhere."

He strapped on his gladius and attached his bow and quiver to his saddle. While he was fiddling with the buckles, he growled, "And bring that leather wrapping to me. It's under my bed."

I sighed on the inside, rather than out loud. It wasn't the right time to test Nik's patience. I dismounted and did as I was told.

"I took this off the leader, boy", he said. "It's a gift. A reward for all the effort you've put into your training." He abruptly turned around and started walking his horse down the road.

I placed the package on the ground and unwrapped the oiled leather cover. Inside was a Roman shortsword. I realised that it was no ordinary military issue sword. I could hardly believe it. With a trembling hand I lifted the blade by its leather-wrapped hilt. It was still a bit too heavy, but I could wield it, though with difficulty. The blade was perfectly balanced. I would ask Nik about this weapon. I wrapped it again reverently, tied it to my saddle, and trotted off to catch up to the old man.

I found Nik a few moments later. He had dismounted and was kneeling beside a pile of stones. "Are you just going to sit there and think about your new sword or are you going to help me?" he growled.

I jumped off the horse and gave Nik a bear hug. "Thank you Nik, it is unbelievable."

"Bah… it's just a sword… now help me and stop behaving like a girl."

A third of a watch later the cuts on my hands were bleeding and a sizeable pile of rocks lay next to Nik's feet. I removed yet another rock, revealing the lid of a wooden chest. I cleared the last of the stones away and Nik helped me to lift the chest from the hole. He opened the lid. Never in my life had I seen so many gold coins. There must have been enough gold to buy one hundred estates such as the one we had worked on.

Nik handed me three leather pouches. "Fill them up properly and put the chest back. You had better mark this spot in your mind, boy. Next time I might not be here to show you where to dig."

Chapter 3 – Procurator

We arrived at the city of Sirmium before nightfall.

Labourers, merchants and travellers tend to crowd city gates at dusk, preferring to spend the night within the relative safety of the walls. The gates usually close at sunset. Only the privilege of rank or the application of a generous bribe to the watch officer would get them to open just wide enough for one to slip in. Alternatively, one spends the night outside, which comes with its own set of risks.

We were four hundred paces from the gate when Nik gave me a nudge and said, "Relax boy, let me handle this. We don't want them to search us and confiscate the gold."

Our appearance was typical of Roman settlers, which the Romanised barbarians tended to imitate. Any doubt was removed from the mind of the duty guards when Nik greeted them in perfect Latin. Shaving one's hair and wearing Roman clothes is easy, but acquiring a patrician accent is close to impossible for the average barbarian.

It's strange how people are somehow set at ease by shared ethnicity. There was no real looming threat to the city, so the duty centurion did not afford us more than a cursory glance. The local Pannonians walking behind us were stopped for a full search. It's always more fun to terrorise people if they don't look or speak like your mother or cousin. Anyway, that helped to get us off the hook. Bad luck for the locals, though.

To my surprise, Nik knew his way around the city. We walked in silence along the cobbled streets. Nik kept quiet because he was scheming. I kept quiet because it was my first time in a city and I was completely overwhelmed. Some memories stick, who knows why. I clearly remember that we passed a tavern with a picture of a rearing horse, a grizzled old man with one eye missing leaning against the door frame. Weird. That and the terrible smell of shit. That's what I remember.

The farther we walked into the city, the more the neighbourhood improved. The smell of shit became less prominent and the streets became cleaner and less cluttered. More soldiers patrolled the streets. "We are getting closer to the place that we need to visit", Nik said as he stopped in front of an inn that looked too upmarket to suit our ragged appearance. Two huge brutes flanked the entrance to the courtyard. I had no doubt that their loose clothing concealed weapons. Nik exchanged a few words with them, and a couple of heartbeats later one of the guards appeared with a well-groomed individual in tow. I assumed he was the innkeeper. He did not seem overly keen to deal with us. Nik took the man aside, spoke softly, and produced a gold coin. That made all the difference in the world.

Nik addressed the innkeeper with an air of authority, bordering on arrogance. "We need a comfortable room for at least two nights, with stabling for six horses. Good food and good wine for me and my son. Arrange for a tailor to be brought to us within the hour." Before the innkeeper could answer, Nik produced another gold aureus. He did not wait for the innkeeper to respond, but entered the inn. The innkeeper, whose body language had changed from haughty to subservient, hurried past us and led us to a grand room with a small balcony. "Leave us", Nik said gruffly.

That day Nik unknowingly taught me a valuable lesson concerning the worth of gold.

The tailor arrived within a third of a watch. He took our measurements and promised to have our new tunics and wool cloaks ready by sunrise. He would have to work all night. For the right amount of gold, one can persuade men to do almost anything.

Nik woke me early. The inn had its own baths where we were oiled and cleaned by slaves. Nik ordered a shave and we both had our hair trimmed - all administered by willing slaves. Our new clothes were neatly laid out on the soft mattresses by the time we arrived back at our room.

I was amazed at what could be achieved by a couple of small gold coins. I still am, sometimes.

"Lucius, dress yourself in the white cloak and the thin tunic", Nik said. "Make it quick, we have a lot to do today".

A hearty breakfast was laid out on the table on the balcony. Cold pork roast and freshly baked bread with honey and olives. Nik ordered two mugs of watered white wine of an unknown vintage. We gorged on the rich feast. Afterwards, slaves appeared with wet towels to wipe our hands and faces.

I followed Nik into the busy street. He walked with a determined stride.

We did not have far to travel, and soon came to a halt in front of an impressive stone building in the forum. It was well-guarded, with at least half a dozen heavily armed legionaries standing to attention.

Nik walked to the guard at the entrance and said, "I need to see the procurator."

"Do you have an official appointment?" the guard replied.

"No, but…", was as far as Nik got.

The guard cut him off mid-sentence. "Stuff off then, grandpa, before you get yourself arrested."

Nik was not put off so easily. He produced a silver coin, handed it to the guard and said, "Please, call the clerk of the procurator. I am a personal friend of Sextus Condianus."

The guard remained motionless for a span of heartbeats, obviously weighing up the benefit of the coin against the possible punishment of disturbing the procurator unnecessarily. I knew by then that the silver would be effective, which it was.

Shortly afterwards we stood in the office of the clerk of the procurator. He was clearly Greek, as all good administrators tend to be. The clerk had a bored look about him – no doubt used to turn down people who desired an audience with the most important man in Pannonia Inferior. He started to recite his reply without emotion when Nik passed him two gold coins. Nik then addressed him in perfect Greek, "Go tell the procurator that the Olympian is here to see him. He will see me. Just do it. He will be most annoyed if he discovers that you have refused me."

The clerk reflected for a heartbeat. It might have been the thought of enraging the procurator, or it could have been the bribe, but he decided to comply. "My employer is extremely busy", the clerk said. "I will inform him of your request, but I doubt that he will be able to accommodate you. Wait here." With that he turned on his heel and marched out of the office.

Not sixty heartbeats had passed when we were escorted into the opulently decorated office of Procurator Sextus Quintilius Condianus. We were left standing awkwardly in the centre of the huge room. The clerk entered and remained next to the door. The procurator followed, escorted by two muscular guards. He seemed of the same age as Nik, the only difference being that he displayed less wear and tear, most probably due to a more pampered life. He squinted, then wiped his eyes. "By all the gods, man, is it really you?"

"Leave us", Condianus said. The guards exchanged glances and started to object, but a hand signal from the procurator was enough to crush any resistance.

The procurator waited until he was sure the guards had left the passage, then walked to the door and closed it.

He ignored me and spoke to Nik. "I was told you were dead. To be honest, I reckoned they had taken care of you."

Nik smiled slyly. "I suppose that didn't worry you overmuch?"

"I always respected you, especially afterwards. But no, I didn't worry too much. It seemed that all the loose ends were tied up", Condianus replied.

Nik smiled again. "You know, I still have the letter after all these years. Safely hidden, of course, and in perfect condition. Your signature is second from the top on the left. They must have searched for me for years. Found me yesterday. They are all dead, though."

Condianus's appearance changed, and a nervous twitch settled in a corner of his mouth. "Why are you here then? Name your price."

"As you know, I am a reasonable man", Nik replied. "Sometimes petty, but let's leave that for now. What I require is easy, and it will ensure that you may live in peace for the rest of your life, instead of providing entertainment for the crowd in the Flavian Amphitheatre."

"The killers sent by your friends murdered the owner of the estate I lived on. His name was Quintus Domitius Aurelianus, a Roman citizen who settled and married a local woman. He served in the Legio III Italica for twenty-five years, and obtained the rank of centurion. Quintus had no family apart from those who were killed. He was a good man and should not have died in vain."

Nik placed his hand on my shoulder and said, "This boy is named Lucius. When we leave this office, he will have a copy of the official documents showing him to be Lucius Domitius Aurelianus. The son and heir of Quintus. His estates will be left untended until he wishes to return and take ownership. Until then the government of Pannonia Inferior will rent it from him for an amount equal to one gold aureus per month, payable when he provides proof of identity at this office."

I was listening to this with my mouth wide open, struggling to grasp the enormity of the situation.

Nik stood, walked to the desk, and poured himself a silver goblet of rich red wine. He left it unwatered, which is the barbarian way.

"This is all I ask. It is as nothing to you, this I know. In return, the boy and I will disappear. I will not return to Roman territory. Not ever. The boy will only return after your death, if he ever has that desire."

Chapter 4 – Ride to Viminacium

It was late afternoon when all the documents were completed and stamped with the official seal of the procurator. We hurried from his office, and Nik whispered, "Lucius, we leave Sirmium immediately."

We made a brief detour to collect the horses and pack our few belongings before bribing our way through the gates. Although bordering on the insane, we rode at a canter with only the moon illuminating the road.

"I have known Sextus Condianus for years", Nik said. "He is mostly an honourable man. Mostly. He is also a pragmatist and he might view our demise as the best and least risky way of resolving this issue. Let's ride as if he has dispatched a turma of auxiliary cavalry to deal with us."

The fear of death is a very handy tool to banish the aches, pains and fatigue of riding hours on end without rest. We changed horses often. They weren't the best horseflesh in Pannonia, but they were well rested and even better fed. When the sun crested the horizon, we practically flew. I learned to ride before I could walk. Nik was a superb horseman, although his age probably made it a challenge.

We rode in silence. Nik knew where we were going, or rather, I was convinced he knew. As if reading my thoughts, he said,

"They would expect us to cross the Danube at Onagrinum, which is twenty miles north of Sirmium. An auxiliary cohort guards the ferry crossing. Rather, we will travel due east to Viminacium in Moesia which is about one hundred and twenty miles east of Sirmium. I estimate that we have travelled twenty-five miles during the night, and another twenty this morning. We will have to rest and water the horses by noon."

We kept to the Roman road, passing travellers, farmers and countless peasants. The province was at peace, and none bothered to give us a second glance. Is it not strange how peasants are always on the road, travelling to some unknown destination, even without a horse or baggage?

Come noon, we left the roadway after crossing a small stream, and walked the horses until we were hidden from sight by scrubby trees. We watered the horses and hobbled them, to be safe. I lay down in the tall grass and almost immediately fell into a deep sleep. I woke up a full watch later. Nik was snoring next to me, wrapped in his cloak. I didn't try to touch him. Even I learn from my mistakes, believe it or not. I retreated to a safe distance and threw a not-so-small stone against his back, with a bit more force than intended. He woke up, looked at me, clearly annoyed, stretched, and stood up slowly like the old man he was.

"If we leave immediately and keep up a good pace, we could be in Singidunum before nightfall", Nik stated as a fact, and handed me a meat sausage, left over from our stay in Sirmium. "Eat this while you ride."

At dusk we passed by Singidunum, where the road widened to eight paces. He shouted to be heard over the noise of the hooves on the road, "We are now travelling on the Via Militaris. This road was built to allow mass deployment of troops should the barbarians attack any of the forts along the border fortifications. You can see the construction is superior to the road we travelled on before. We will be able to ride faster on this road. We ride until a watch after sunset. Then we rest."

By the time Nik called a halt, I was ready to collapse. I nearly did during the last mile. Maybe that was why Nik acted. Falling off a cantering horse on a paved road can be a serious setback to one's health.

I nearly fell from the horse and was so weary that I had trouble walking. Nik wasn't in much better shape. We camped in the forest and decided to light a fire to prepare a meal. Dry wood was freely available and I had a fire going in no time. We concocted a stew with lightly smoked pork, leftover meat sausage, onion and garlic. It tasted delicious with the stale bread Nik conjured from his pack. If you are really, really hungry and tired, anything warm and half edible will taste straight out of Elysium.

* * *

"Wake up boy, it's time to ride. Just one more watch and we will be in Viminacium", Nik said, and rose stiffly.

We finished off the leftovers of the stew and stale bread. Although the sun wasn't visible yet, it was light enough to ride at a gallop.

Chapter 5 – Crossing the limes

Viminacium was an impressive sight.

The thick stone walls of the legionary fortress were studded with massive towers, and rose to the height of three men. Even from a mile away I could see the multitude of legionaries patrolling the battlements.

"Lucius, Rome is a mighty empire and has been at peace for a long time. But don't be fooled. On the other side of these borders are barbarian tribes fiercer and more terrible than you can imagine. Fearsome warriors who fight from childhood, and who are used to enduring the worst. Their numbers are like the stars in the sky - thousands upon thousands. The only barrier between them and us are these fortifications. Thousands of miles of stone and earthen walls keep the barbarians from flooding into the Empire. Rome is able to mobilise thirty-three legions and more than four hundred auxiliary regiments, meaning nearly half a million soldiers. Most of them defend our borders. Not unlike what you see here today."

I was afforded a glimpse of the might of the Roman army. The presence of a single legion and the enormous fortress blew my mind. But thousands of miles of walls, ditches, embankments, towers and tens of thousands of heavily armed men in steel?

That was too much to imagine. How could one people build such military might, and how on earth could it be sustained?

Nik quickly brought me back from my reverie. "Lucius, we need to get across the Danube, and we have to do it now. Our lives are in danger until we leave civilisation behind."

We made our way through the gated fortifications that gave access to the port at Viminacium.

Although the *limes* was meant to protect us from the wild hordes north of the river, this part of the world had not seen a hostile barbarian for a very long time. It is not dissimilar to having a friend with a vicious dog. After visiting him a couple of times at his house without seeing or hearing the dog, one assumes that the animal has either become docile or is not there anymore. Then one day the dog attacks you when you least expect it. The same applies to barbarians. The key is to remain vigilant and expect trouble, but men are men. The legionary officers at the port operated like merchants. Trade with the barbarians was booming, and all was well. Coin was being made and nobody queried why Nik was arranging a berth across the river.

Nik soon found a barge captain willing to ferry us and our mounts across the mighty Danube. Two gold coins ensured an immediate departure.

At first sight, the river took my breath away - ten times wider than any I had seen before. Nearly half a mile across. We anchored on the northern bank, and as the captain secured the ropes to the quay, Nik paid him. He couldn't stop smiling, and kept rubbing the coins in his grubby hands. It was a good deal for everyone. We felt safe for the first time in many days.

How wrong we were.

Chapter 6 – Barbaricum

Nik visibly relaxed after we had crossed the Danube. Barbaricum was a well-known sanctuary for anyone who had had a disagreement with the Roman Empire.

"Lucius, we are in the lands of the Yazyges, an ancient Sarmatian tribe. They used to be nomadic, but nowadays they seem to prefer living in villages. They have a love-hate relationship with Rome. Sometimes they are Rome's client kingdom, forming a buffer against us and other barbarian races. At other times they become discontent with the relationship and raid deep into Roman territory. Last time that happened, Emperor Caracalla defeated them. That was ten years ago. Who knows what the current situation is, but I have a feeling we are soon to find out."

"Some will even tell you that we are still in Roman controlled territory, but I laugh at that statement. If that was the case, why would Viminacium be heavily fortified?"

There was a Yazyges village close to where we disembarked from the ferry. In contrast to Viminacium, stone buildings were glaringly absent, and all that could be seen were a number of dilapidated wooden structures and an assortment of tents. I think there were more Romans in the village than Yazyges. Or rather, they appeared more Roman than barbarian. Most of the folk could speak Latin, which was not surprising as they lived in such close proximity to Viminacium. A good portion of the frontier trade of goods and slaves must have passed through this settlement.

Given the fact that even the savages spoke Latin, we had no trouble to purchase what we needed for the journey. Fresh and smoked meat, cheese, freshly baked bread, olives and grain. Nik even managed to buy four amphorae of red wine, and last but not least, a small leather tent.

We decided not to stay in the village and provide one of the Romanised barbarians with the opportunity to steal back all the provisions we had bought.

A full watch before sunset we departed, heading north, away from the far-reaching influence of the Empire, towards the undisputed tribal lands of the Yazyges. We kept to a Roman road which probably used to be in good condition, long, long ago. But enough complaining, it was still useable and better than a trackless hinterland.

It was our seventh day on the road. Nik and I felt relaxed, riding at a leisurely pace, passing the odd traveller. All was well again.

Sometimes the gods speak to us, they give us direction, but it happens without us realising. This was one of those times. I looked over my shoulder for no apparent reason. We were close to the foothills of the mountains and therefore the landscape became increasingly undulating. The road was visible where it crested several low hills in both directions. My eye caught the sun reflecting off metal, but I did not know what to make of it. Fortunately I had the clarity of mind to mention it to Nik immediately.

"Keep up, boy", he shouted, and we galloped along the road to the top of the hill that we were ascending. We reined in beside a lone tree at the side of the road. Motionlessly we watched. Less than one hundred heartbeats later we saw a column of horsemen, maybe twenty, galloping with purpose in our direction.

"What you see, boy, is Roman legionary cavalry. Damn, they are coming for us. Damn. Ride boy, forget the packhorse and bring the remounts. Ride for your life. We still have a chance."

Nik left the Roman road at the first opportunity, with me following close on his heels. The hilly country was scattered with rocky outcrops and shrubs, interspersed with the occasional copse of small trees. We didn't follow a road, just desperately galloped away as fast as the terrain allowed. I estimated the Romans to be about a mile behind us. That meant they would be aware of the fact that we had left the road, and were close on our heels.

We rode like madmen, crossed a low hill, and came upon a path of sorts. Nik immediately started down the track at speed. The countryside flattened out and soon we were riding along a narrow valley. The quality of the cavalry horses was far superior to our own. It was especially noticeable on the flat, even terrain. Our pursuers narrowed the gap with every stride. I risked a glimpse over my shoulder. They were less than three hundred paces behind us. Our prospects looked bleak. They would catch us.

It is indeed strange how the mind works. I have been in situations like this often enough to notice it. When faced with imminent death, the mind elevates itself and somehow becomes 'sharper'. You see things much clearer, and in a different way, like walking from fog into daylight.

Remaining atop the horse while riding at a gallop required all my concentration. From the corner of my eye I picked up movement – nine horsemen wearing loose-fitting woollen robes and leggings. I shouted to Nik, but do not remember the words. For a heartbeat I thought they intended to intercept us, but then noticed that their stares were fixed on our pursuers. The strange men rode with a speed and agility that I thought impossible. Without breaking stride, they drew their Scythian bows from their saddles and nocked arrows.

The Roman cavalrymen were so intent on catching their prey that they only became aware of the danger moments before the first flight of arrows was released. The effect was devastating. Within the space of two heartbeats, the horsemen had each expensed three shafts. To the credit of the Romans, they did not panic. They advanced towards the attackers and hefted stabbing spears in their right hands, while shields protected their bodies from arrows. A hundred paces from the Romans, the Scythians swerved skilfully, and fled in the opposite direction. The tribesmen were masters in the art of horse archery - of the initial twenty-five Romans, only twelve were left. The retreating horsemen turned in their saddles and released arrows at the Romans over the rumps of their horses with deadly accuracy.

I spotted another, smaller group of Scythians, about half a dozen, trotting towards the skirmish. They were shielded from the view of the Roman cavalry by the retreating archers and the dust they created. These men were mounted on magnificent horses - muscular, big brutes. Their riders carried thick-shafted spears, eight feet long, which they gripped with both hands. The line of archers parted, allowing the heavy spearmen to pass through seamlessly.

Heartbeats later the wall of metal and horseflesh struck the line of Roman horsemen with an audible clash. I remember witnessing one of the long, heavy spears pass straight through a cavalryman wearing chain armour, like a hot dagger slicing through butter.

When the dust had settled, all that remained of our pursuers were mangled corpses.

Chapter 7 – Confession

We felt like spectators in the Flavium Amphitheatre. I risked a glance in Nik's direction. He was stealing me a glance. We both grinned.

A couple of heartbeats earlier we were fleeing for our lives. Now we were watching our saviours finish off our pursuers and looting the bodies.

The Scythians ignored us. Looting was important. We were going nowhere.

When a quarter of a watch had passed, having finished their business, the Scythians congregated. Following a brief discussion, they walked their horses in our direction. There was no hostility or aggression. The group came to a halt about ten paces away.

"Twenty-five men, attacking old warrior and boy. No honour. They deserved die", one of the Scythians said in broken Latin.

Then Nik surprised me again. He spoke to the Scythians in their own language. They were as surprised as I was.

Nik spoke with them for a while. There was a lot of nodding and smiling from the Scythians and Nik said, "Lucius, we are going to travel with them. We will be safe."

I nodded and followed the old man, who turned his horse to the east.

Nik and our new friends exchanged a few words occasionally, but in general, they left us to ourselves.

I had ample time to study them, but tried not to stare openly. They were tall men with blonde hair and thick blonde beards. Broad in the shoulders and strong - not heavyset like most gladiators, but muscular in a sinewy way. The build one acquires from spending one's days in the saddle while hunting and training with weapons. They were handsome, jovial men who laughed and spoke continuously.

Then Nik enlightened me. "During my years in Rome, I made only one really good friend. He is an Alani, or to be more specific, a Roxolani. Our rescuers are from the same tribe. They told me that my old friend is still alive, and a very important man in their lands. We are travelling to visit him. These men are our friends and they will protect us."

The Roxolani were on their way back to their tribal lands after successfully trading with the Yazyges. They were in no hurry.

I don't remember much about the journey to where the Roxolani made their home. I do remember that we rode east and then north for at least half a moon, crossing various streams and rivers.

The tribesmen kept mostly to themselves. Nik brooded. He was clearly irritated, and therefore I was reluctant to speak with him.

Early one evening, following three days of relative silence, we sat beside the cooking fire in front of our tent. A small buck was roasting over the flames. Nik had brought it down earlier in the day with a well-aimed arrow. Our friends had their own fire and were already deep into their cups, as was the case most evenings.

Nik was sipping from his third cup of unwatered wine when he broke the silence. "Lucius, stop fiddling with the meat. Come sit down next to me. We need to talk."

I sensed his serious mood and did as I was told. I was trying to ensure that our meat didn't burn, but if talking could get Nik out of his dark mood, so be it.

"You asked me a while ago who the men were who attacked us on the farm", he said. "I could not tell you until we far removed from their grasp. We are safe now, so I have no reason not to share it with you. Unfortunately it is not a short answer. Listen to what I tell you and listen carefully."

Nik filled his own cup and told his tale.

"I was born in the last year of the reign of Emperor Antoninus Pius. It was an unusually peaceful time in the history of the

Empire. There were no wars during the twenty years preceding my birth. When I was only a year old, the emperor died in his sleep and was succeeded by Marcus Aurelius. Marcus Aurelius was a good man and an even better emperor. My father, a senator, knew him well and mostly praised his actions. The emperor was a thinker and a philosopher. His son was born at the same time as me, and he named him Lucius."

"Marcus Aurelius ensured that Lucius received all the intellectual tutoring that time allowed for. He even appointed his physician, Galen, to arrange and oversee the tutoring. Galen sourced tutors and intellectuals from the far reaches of the Empire. None refusing the opportunity to mould the future ruler of the world. Speaking and writing in Latin, Greek and Arabic, his father also made sure that he had a rudimentary understanding of the Germanic languages. He was extremely intelligent, therefore he excelled."

"When the emperor's son was twelve summers old, Marcus Aurelius realised that the boy was physically gifted. He could run faster than his peers, was stronger, excelled at weapons training and won all the wrestling bouts. His father never possessed those physical talents and I think he hoped that if he could raise a child that had knowledge and could fight like a demigod, Rome would benefit."

"As a reward for his academic progress and achievements, he instructed Galen to procure experts to assist with his son's martial training. Galen employed swordsmen from Spain and Germany, archers and horsemen from Scythia and wrestlers from Greece. Lucius excelled, but he was unhappy. He had no friends to share it with."

"During that time Marcus Aurelius approached my father. I was of the same age as Lucius and showed a talent for most things of a physical nature. The Emperor requested that I visit the palace every day for four hours to be a training partner to his son."

"There was never really a choice with such a request. Even a humble man like Marcus Aurelius was not to be refused. The ruler of the world gets what he desires."

"I started training the very next day. Lucius was a likeable boy, and we got along from the very start. He had been training with the instructors for a couple of months already, so I had to catch up. The training was tough. I trained with the bow until my fingers bled. Trained with the sword until I couldn't lift my arms. Yes, arms, boy. If you want to be a proper archer or swordsman, you need to be able to use the weapon with both your hands."

"In any event, we trained, trained and trained some more. We became good friends. We duelled with wooden swords and wrestled. Wrestling was my forte."

"I had just turned fifteen when I beat Lucius at wrestling for the first time. I still remember that day clearly. Lucius slowly stood up from the sand of the gymnasium, grasped my forearm in the military way and said, 'Well done Narcissus, excellent technique.' But his eyes told a different story. He looked at me in a different way that day, and I realised that I had made a mistake. The boy was not my friend. He was the future emperor. From that day onwards I always allowed him to win. I think he knew, but he expected that of me."

"Lucius, turn the spit. I don't wish to eat charcoal tonight", Nik growled.

I was brought back to reality with a shock. Obediently I turned the meat. It had burnt already, but we could just cut it away. I poured Nik another cup of wine without him asking, and sat down next to him.

"Thank you Lucius, there is still hope for you", Nik winked.

He continued.

"Round about this time, Lucius was elevated to Caesar, which meant that he was the heir apparent to the emperor."

"Lucius slowly became a different person after the official appointment. We were ordered to address him as 'Caesar Lucius' and he became increasingly distant. We were still friends, but our friendship became stiff, even to the point of being formal. Not unlike a master who befriends his slave."

"I guess I was searching for a true friend as well and I grew close to the archery instructor. He was called Apsikal, a Roxolani prince by birth, and my senior by a few years. In return for providing his services to Rome, he received tutoring from a Greek tutor called Nikophoros. I used to join him for the lessons. We were not allowed to receive the same tutoring as 'Caesar Lucius'. I think that he was at a too high level to accommodate us mere mortals."

"Barbarians make much better friends than Romans. Romans, especially patricians, are taught from birth to deceive. Roxolani are brought up with honour. They would think nothing of giving their life for a friend. I pleaded with Apsikal not to show me any favour during training as I knew that it would enrage Lucius."

"We continued our martial training even after Lucius had started attending the College of Pontiffs. That, young Lucius, is where they show future rulers how to be the Pontifex Maximus, the chief priest of Rome."

"Lucius and I became experts at archery, horse archery, swordplay and wrestling. We also trained to fight with daggers and with our fists only. We were fifteen and we were killers - educated killers mind you."

"Marcus Aurelius became ill shortly afterwards. It wasn't public knowledge. He knew he had only two or three years to live. He fast-tracked his son's career. Lucius was appointed as joint ruler with Marcus Aurelius and renamed Caesar Lucius Aurelius Commodus Antoninus Augustus. Bit of a mouthful, eh…?"

"And it went straight to his head. Just like Marcus Aurelius hadn't planned."

"Lucius got married as well. Bruttia Crispina. I attended the wedding ceremony. It was a modest affair, but commemoration coins were minted nonetheless. She was from an influential, rich and powerful family, and ugly as shit. Shame. I couldn't help to pity Lucius, although he deserved it."

"My friend the co-emperor started to travel with his father, the tutors and trainers in tow. I joined them."

"Lucius was occupied with things that required the attention of an emperor and I spent most of my time refining my archery skills with Apsikal."

"While we were touring the Danubian frontier, Marcus Aurelius became very ill. We all knew that his time to cross the river had arrived. He knew it as well, and tried to spend most of his remaining time with his son. Coaching and tutoring him and giving advice. All wasted time in the end. How sad."

"The great man passed away two days after the Ides of March. And my friend Lucius became the emperor."

"Commodus's first action as sole emperor was to bribe the barbarians on the other side of the river. He called it a peace treaty. We returned to Rome and he arranged a triumph in honour of himself. I found it distasteful. Where the philosopher Marcus Aurelius had conquered with the sword, the killer Commodus conquered with bribes. It felt wrong."

"When we arrived back in Rome and all the triumphal dust had settled, our lives changed. Apsikal was appointed to the personal bodyguard of Commodus and I ended up starting a new life. I didn't get to see Commodus much, but we made an arrangement to meet once a month to train together. Surprisingly he honoured most of our appointments."

"From discussions with Commodus and Apsikal, I realised that the new emperor wasn't interested in Rome at all. All he was interested in was to race horses and chariots and fight in the Flavium Amphitheatre. Well, he was good at that at least."

"Commodus, due to his disinterest in government, appointed Greek administrators to run the Empire on his behalf. Pretty soon there was a power struggle between the Greek administrators, the Praetorians, Marcia his mistress, successful generals, to name but a few. I kept out of this. I had my occasional cup of wine with Apsikal and my occasional bout of training with Commodus. And I heard the rumours in the corridors."

"Twelve years after he became emperor, things took a turn for the worse. Commodus became completely insane. He believed that he was a god. He truly believed it, he told me."

"He declared himself the founder of Rome, changing Rome's name. By the gods, he even changed the names of the months of the year to correspond to his twelve names. He saw a conspiracy behind every bush and killed innocent senators on a whim. It was a disgrace to Rome and an insult to his father's name."

"So, inevitably, he was poisoned by Marcia, his mistress. But it gets more interesting. She didn't do a proper job. Typical, eh?"

"Commodus knew he had been poisoned. While he was recuperating from the ordeal, he made a list of everyone he would kill once he had fully recovered. Lists are always good things. The gods forbid you have to kill people later, who, at first, escaped your mind. It gets messy."

"Anyway, while he was getting better, the list accidentally fell into the hands of Marcia via a child. Marcia's name was at the top of the list. My father's name was in the top ten, and even Apsikal's, for not discovering the perpetrators before they struck. The rest of the list contained most of the names of the old and respected senators and military commanders. Commodus didn't suffer failure."

"Apsikal came to me that evening. I immediately sensed that something was very wrong. He was distraught. I ushered him into the study, for privacy, and he told me the story in his accented Latin. When I realised where it was going, I produced an amphora of excellent red to calm the nerves. He had given years of his life to train and protect the emperor. Now Apsikal was to die at his hands. Commodus had clearly lost his mind. He was destroying himself, and even worse, he was destroying Rome and the legacy of the great man, Marcus Aurelius."

"Lucius was a good friend. Commodus was a monster. We had to stop him. I sent Apsikal back to Marcia with a message. I would deal with Commodus, but in return I required a large sum in gold and a letter signed by the real conspirators. I believe in insurance."

"When your name is on the assassination list of Commodus, you see things in a different light. Most of the senators would never, ever sign anything that could incriminate them in any way. But this was different, they were dead already and only I could bring them back to life."

"I was probably the only person who could go to Commodus's rooms without being turned away, or killed if he was in a mood. And they knew it."

"Two-thirds of a watch later I walked to the palace with Apsikal at my side. The gold was at my house and the letter signed and secured. I was going to kill a friend and save Rome."

"I was allowed entry into the palace without question. To annoy a friend of Commodus meant certain death. I was briefly stopped by the guards at the door, but Commodus waved them away and let me enter."

"Against my better judgement, I had decided to talk to Commodus, in case a bit of the old Lucius remained. Maybe, just maybe I could talk him out of it. Commodus walked towards me, called me brother, and opened his arms to embrace me. I immediately knew something was amiss, as he was never that familiar. The room was dark, only illuminated by a couple of oil lamps. My tutors would have been proud of me that evening. I remembered them mentioning that if you have to kill, dispense with the small talk. And I did. He never saw it coming. I struck him on the windpipe with the outside of my open right hand, just below the chin. A killing blow. Just like that. The concealed dagger that he wanted to put into my back dropped from his hand and he crumpled to the floor."

"I dragged the body to the bed and sat down on the edge to gather my thoughts. Killing was never something that unsettled me. I really just wanted to make up time to ensure no one asked questions. I covered his body with a thin blanket, walked through the door, and closed it behind me. I explained to the guards that Commodus wished not to be disturbed."

"I left the palace immediately. I didn't waste any time to tell Marcia. I hurried to my house where Apsikal was waiting for me with four horses. I might be a murderer, but I am not stupid. I knew I would be blamed and that they would come for me, and probably for Apsikal as well."

"The horses were magnificent. Excellent horses suitable for long distance riding. Apsikal knew horses. I think he could speak horse."

"As soon as we had exited the gates of the city we practically flew."

"I was one of the best horsemen in the Empire, and Apsikal was better by far. No one had any hope of ever catching us. We headed for the lands of the Scythians. Apsikal's lands."

"Lucius, take the meat off the fire, you're ruining it", the old man grunted.

I took the buck off the spit and placed the steaming meat beside the fire. Nik passed me balls of wheat dough he had prepared earlier. I retrieved hot stones from the fire, flattened the dough, and waited for the flatbread to cook.

Nik cut the most succulent pieces of meat from the fillet of the buck and passed me a piece of hard cheese. The fresh bread and meat were delicious, and I washed it down with water, fortified with a bit of red wine. I had a lot to think about, it's not every day that you find out your caregiver killed the ruler of the known world.

"Lucius, my tale is not finished yet", Nik said. "But it's all for tonight. You will find out soon why I couldn't tell you any of this earlier."

I don't remember my reply. What could a child say anyway after hearing that tale? I do remember having terrible nightmares of emperors, killing, and flight. No surprise there, I guess.

One thing I have learned over the years is that there is no peace to be had in telling a child an incomplete story.

As we rode the next day, I kept bothering Nik. "So how long did it take you to find Apsikal's people?" I asked. "What colour was the horse you rode on? Can I still call you Nik?" and a myriad of other questions.

Chapter 8 – The story continues

We still had food left over from the previous evening. I took slices of meat from my bag, seasoned it with salt, and stacked it onto the two remaining flatbreads. Nik produced a handful of olives, a round of hard cheese, and a small pot of honey.

When we had licked the last of the honey from our fingers, I poured Nik a beaker of the wine he loved and added a little to my water.

The old man wetted his throat and continued.

"They never had a chance to catch us, and they never did. Years later I heard the rumour that I had been caught and executed. As you can see, that never happened."

"We eventually found Apsikal's people and were warmly welcomed. His father was the king of the tribe, and a powerful man. Apsikal was the heir apparent, the eldest son. He had no other siblings competing for the throne, but he had a younger sister. I stayed with them for years, becoming one of the tribe."

I saw a strange sadness appear in Nik's eyes. He took a deep swallow of the wine and I filled his nearly empty cup to the brim.

Nik nodded his appreciation. "I fell in love with her, but kept it a secret for many years. She never married - I suspect for the same reason. Eventually things developed between us, but I knew that her father would not approve, as I was a Roman by birth and many years older than her. The king soon realised the truth of the matter. In most cases it would not be a problem, as he would just have me killed discreetly, but he took a liking to me. He probably viewed me as the one who brought his prodigal son back to him. I was a warrior, the equal to any of his champions, except maybe Apsikal, and the king respected it. My relationship with the princess caused divisions within the tribe, but I did not have an answer to our dilemma."

"One morning Apsikal woke me before sunrise."

"'My sister is waiting for you at the river crossing, with horses', he said. 'Go now if you want to live. When I am king, come back, brother, and there will be a place of honour for you at my side.' He embraced me and I left without packing."

"Aritê was waiting for me at the river, with four horses. And half of the gold, the blood money. It was still a king's ransom, even if it were half."

"We crossed the Danube and reached Sirmium without incident. We rested at an inn and decided to take passage to

Africa. Too many people knew me in the big cities. I would be discovered and brought to book. Due to the heavy traffic on the Roman road, we kept to the hills."

"That's when our path crossed with Quintus. Half a dozen bandits attacked him on his way back from the market. He had an arrow in his shoulder, and had fallen off his cart. I carried my bow with me, a gift from the king of the Roxolani. It was a massacre, like swatting flies. Aritê didn't even join in. Did I mention she was better with the bow than me? That's another story."

"Anyway, I killed all the bandits with my bow, from the saddle, without even breaking a sweat."

"We decided to take Quintus home, nurse him back to health and then move on to Alexandria in Egypt. The gods had other plans. Aritê became with child. I was the father. Quintus was a good man, a retired man of the legions, and honourable. We made a deal with him. In return for saving his life, we would be allowed to stay on the farm and he would take care of us like family."

"I insisted on working on the farm, not as a slave, but as a freedman. I thoroughly enjoyed it, and took pride in my work."

"Then the gods intervened again. A life for a life, but I would have given mine instead. The strong, beautiful Aritê died while giving birth."

Nik's eyes were moist, his head buried in his hands.

"But the gods gave me a second chance, a chance to make good on my mistakes."

"Lucius, you are the son of Aritê and Narcissus. You are my son. If people knew the truth, they would have killed you too when they came for me."

So what do you say to that?

I had always looked up to Nik like I would to a father. His revelation only made me feel good, not cheated in any way.

I walked over to Nik, who probably expected a rebuke. I embraced him and said. "Nik, you were always my father, and always will be."

Then we ate in silence, each occupied with their own thoughts, and went to bed.

Chapter 9 – Men of metal

It seemed like we were on the road for months, but I never counted the days. Show me a child that does that kind of thing.

I remember Nik having an animated discussion with the leader of our entourage late one morning. He trotted over to me, dismounted, and said, "Lucius, we wait here. The tribesman will tell King Apsikal that an old friend has come to visit. Custom does not allow anyone to enter the presence of the king of the Roxolani unannounced. No, he either welcomes you or you die. I have not seen Apsikal in nearly twelve years. People change. He might think of me as the Roman who took his sister from him."

Nik didn't say much while we were waiting for news. He was clearly apprehensive.

Mid-afternoon a messenger arrived - the king would be there within the hour. We bathed in the nearby stream and donned our clean tunics and best cloaks. Nik shaved his stubble with the aid of a bronze mirror.

Once we were done, Nik combed my hair and took a step backwards to inspect his handiwork. "Pretty respectable for a boy whose been on the road for weeks", he said.

I had groomed the horses on my father's instruction and he nodded his approval when he noticed their gleaming coats.

The ground began to tremble beneath our feet, announcing the arrival of the king. We had our first good view of the party when they appeared over a low ridge. It was far from the ragtag trading party we met along the road. These were the warrior nobility of the Roxolani.

I was stunned by the sight. The king led the column. He rode a monster of a horse, straw-blonde in colour, with a dark braided mane. The entire head of the horse was encased in riveted bronze plate armour, decorated with intricate etchings. The breast, neck, withers and rump of the horse bristled with thick-woven chain mail, covered with square metal plates of bronze and silver. The saddle was magnificent, red dyed leather decorated with gold inlays, and adorned with buckles of glittering yellow gold.

The king wore a long-sleeved scale armour cuirass of alternating gold and silver scales, which extended to the knees. His vulnerable shins were protected by sculpted golden greaves, buckled onto soft red deerskin boots, and his head adorned with a magnificent pointed helmet of gold, sporting a plume of white horsehair. The brow and nasal guard were made of gilded iron. The back of his neck was protected by thick silver chain mail attached to the bottom of the helmet.

Grey braided hair hung from beneath the rim, and a thick grey plaited beard covered the top of his cuirass.

He wore soft leather gloves, which were reinforced with gold and silver plates on the back.

From the side of his saddle a gold-plated bow protruded from a decorated leather case. A gold-hilted longsword was strapped to his hip.

The sun reflected off the highly polished metal. He shone like a god. Anyway, it was how I imagined a god would look like.

The warriors in his entourage were dressed in the same manner, but none outshone the king.

The great man halted ten paces from where we were standing in the road.

Suddenly I felt very vulnerable. These were warriors, hard men, barbarians.

The king dismounted, and although the action was smooth, I realised that he was no longer a young man. He removed his helmet and handed it to an underling. He walked straight to Nik and embraced him in a bear hug, lifting him into the air with the motion. Both had tears in their eyes and even I could see that the strength of their friendship had not waned during the years of separation.

They stood in an arm's length embrace for a while, exchanging greetings. The king retreated a step or two and shouted a command to his kinsmen. Two saddled horses appeared as if by magic, and he gestured for us to mount and follow him.

Chapter 10 – Camp

I was not sure what to expect. Would there be a fort or a village?

The Roxolani were Scythians, people of the Sea of Grass. This makes them notoriously difficult to conquer. How does one conquer a people without homes, fortresses or buildings?

We rode through a town of wagons and tents. A sizeable town nonetheless. Close to the centre of the settlement, I noticed the magnificent tent of the king rise above the other lesser structures.

Apsikal ushered us into his plush home. On the inside the tent was luxurious. Thick-woven wool carpets covered the floor. All along the walls hung oil lamps. Like in all the other tents, a central hearth provided much needed warmth. Above, an opening in the centre of the tent allowed the smoke to escape. In the tent of the king, servants kept the fire burning all day long. The atmosphere was warm and relaxing. Apsikal issued instructions to the servants in his native tongue and soon golden beakers arrived accompanied by an amphora of dark red wine. Sheep's milk cheese was served on the side.

Barbarians are very different from Romans. If it were a Roman setup, there would have been small talk and then the compulsory deceit. Not so with Apsikal.

"Where is my sister?" he asked. "I miss her."

I realised that Nik was not unaccustomed to the barbarian way. He replied in an equally direct manner. "She died twelve years ago, Apsikal, and with her a part of me died as well."

Until that moment, I had only tagged along like an obedient dog, without being noticed. Abruptly Apsikal turned his gaze on me and spoke to Nik in Latin. "Your son has his mother's eyes. Please introduce me to my nephew."

"Apsikal, this is Lucius, your sister's son. He certainly has his mother's good looks, but the dark hair he inherited from me."

Apsikal turned to face Nik while taking a swallow of the excellent wine. "I trust you understand that this boy here is a prince of the Roxolani. My sons have both perished in battle so I have been left without an heir. The gods have sent you to me, Lucius. You are the future king of the Roxolani."

Neither Nik nor I was prepared for this. Nik wanted to protest, I could see, but he couldn't find the words. I was overwhelmed and just kept quiet, trying to close my gaping mouth. Of course, that was the moment Apsikal chose to study me again. He was confronted by my glazed-over eyes and open maw. I caught a hint of disapproval in his slight frown. He probably thought that he had promised his kingdom to a halfwit.

Well, the whole tone of the evening changed. Apsikal smiled, walked over to Nik, and sat down next to him. The king put his hand on Nik's shoulder and said, "Do not worry old friend, I am not taking your son away from you. He will still be your son. This only means that he will have a new family and an uncle that will care for him like a father."

Apsikal gathered himself and said deliberately, "There is one risk, though. Once people know that he is my closest relative, his life will be in danger. He is too young to defend himself, so we must keep this a secret until the time is right."

From that day on, my life took a different path. I started the year as an orphan. In my own mind the son of a slave girl, not knowing who my father was. A couple of months later, I was the son of the emperor's chosen man and a barbarian princess. And the future ruler of one of the fiercest peoples Rome has ever come into contact with. The Roxolani king could field an army of four thousand heavily armed horse warriors and ten thousand of the best light cavalry the world has ever seen. A bit of a reversal of fortunes, eh? But the gods don't give without receiving. That I know now.

Chapter 11 – Training

When, as a child, you are told that you might be the future king, you involuntarily create a picture in your mind of an easy life, with servants to tend to your every need.

Nothing could have been further from the truth. The Roxolani are a tribe of warriors. War and weapons are their gods. To be a king, you need to be prepared.

Nik explained it to me, and when he had finished, he said, "Only when we are studying written material will we use the language of Rome. From this day onward, you will speak in the Scythian tongue."

Well, that is a bit harsh, I remember thinking.

Apsikal was generous enough to volunteer his champion warrior, a huge brute called Bradakos, as my part-time weapons trainer. Bradakos was a noble, a distant relative of the king. I felt honoured at first, but sadly, the feeling lasted less than a day.

Bradakos, in my humble opinion, was a mean sadist. Or so I believed at the time.

On the first morning Nik took me down to the pasture next to the stream, where Bradakos was waiting impatiently.

He seemed to be in the foulest of moods. I later found out that he was never in a good mood, except when he was killing. That was the only time he smiled.

When I first laid eyes on Bradakos, I thought him to be a servant. The reason being that all the king's companions were adorned in glittering metal armour and carried gilded weapons. Not Bradakos. He was the practical type. He didn't care about fancy armour or shiny swords. All he cared about was to be the most efficient at his job, which was killing, of course.

I stood there, facing him for the first time, not knowing what to expect. I was excited about the prospect of training with sword and spear, like most boys would be.

Bradakos issued instructions to me in Scythian. Someone had obviously forgotten to tell him I didn't speak Scythian.

He turned his back to me and started running in the opposite direction. I was utterly confused. He stopped after about twenty paces, scowled in a desultory way, and slowly walked up to me.

He hit me against the shoulder with an open hand. Looking back, he probably meant it in a clumsy, playful kind of way. I fell onto my side and for a while feared that he had broken my arm. I bit on my teeth, jumped up and ran after him, which was clearly what he wanted me to do.

How could running help me with weapons training? We ran and ran and ran. An hour later I was on all fours, getting rid of my breakfast. And yes, Bradakos was staring at me in amazement, scowl and all. He wasn't even sweating yet.

Every man has his own opinion of cold. To some it's being outside in winter with only a tunic for warmth. To others it's a snowy night without proper furs. I had never known cold until then.

Oblivious to the cold, my trainer removed his tunic and slowly waded into the freezing river. He gestured for me to join him, as he had realised that speaking Scythian to me was a total waste of time. Reluctantly I placed my tunic on the grass and waded into the water. I nearly died, and stopped walking. He looked at me, scowled, and advanced in my direction. I knew what was coming and continued walking. The pain was unbearable. To be fair to him, he did carry me out of the river later on because I had collapsed due to the cold. At least this made me realise that he didn't want to kill me. Or maybe he wanted to, but his loyalty to the king prevented him?

He carried me to the riverbank and rubbed my light blue limbs dry with his cloak. When I was sufficiently revived, Bradakos gestured for me to follow him. We walked along a well-used path until we reached a huge corral with at least forty horses. I assumed they belonged to the king. They were beautiful and well cared for. Huge, powerful beasts. Bradakos said something unintelligible to the men watching over the animals. A short while later they appeared with two saddled horses. We mounted, and rode for miles over the rolling hills of grass. Unlike the running, I was accustomed to it. When we eventually arrived back at the corral, Bradakos gave me a look, not a scowl. I assumed that it was his look of approval.

I followed him to a four-wheeled, covered wagon, close to the king's tent. A woman was bending over a cooking fire, stirring the contents of a sizeable iron cauldron. I wasn't sure whether the woman was Bradakos's slave, wife or mother. He spoke to her in a surprisingly gentle tone and she handed each of us a clay bowl filled with broth. The pottage was meaty, some kind of antelope I assumed because the meat was lean. He motioned for me to eat, which I did, because I was starving. After I had eaten my fill, he took the bowl from me and passed it to the woman for a refill. On handing it back to me I tried to explain to him that I didn't want any more. He laughed gruffly, handed me the bowl, and gestured for me to eat, using the accepted sign. I knew what would happen if I refused, so I forced down the bowl, worried that he would make me eat a third. The second bowl seemed to satisfy him. He handed me a mug of goat milk and gestured 'drink'. I drank the milk, stood, and vomited. Unsurprisingly, Bradakos scowled.

My trainer walked me home, where Nik was waiting for me. Bradakos exchanged a few words with my father, scowled at me, and disappeared.

Nik opened one of the Greek scrolls he used for my tutoring and said in Latin, "Well, Lucius, now that you have had your fun for the day, we need to get some knowledge into that young mind of yours."

I scowled like only a Scythian can. At least I had learned something that day.

I dreaded the weapons training. Although I had yet to touch a weapon of any sorts. Every day the running, swimming and force-feeding continued. Bradakos could not be reasoned with, that I picked up on soon enough.

After six weeks had passed, things changed. I could keep up with Bradakos when it came to running and the water didn't seem that cold anymore. I was beginning to enjoy it. Some days I asked for a third bowl of broth. I felt good. I felt stronger, but I somehow appeared leaner.

One morning, three moons after we had commenced the training, my mentor brought two spear shafts with him. By then I had a rudimentary understanding of the language, and Bradakos and I could communicate in two-word sentences.

He threw me a spear shaft and said, "Come, stand here", gesturing to a spot three paces from where he was standing. He turned my body to face the same direction as his, and growled, "Do what I do."

Well, that was the longest conversation I have had with him up until then and it felt good. He taught me two moves that day. The straight thrust and the parry to the straight thrust. I had to repeat it a thousand times. He could clearly see the boredom and displeasure on my face. When he was satisfied that I had practised it enough, I struggled to lift my hands higher than my chin. Then we ran. I vomited. All too predictable.

I practised the moves and became better at it, or so I thought. After about a moon of the same routine, Bradakos told me to not face forward, but face him during the training.

"You straight thrust, I parry", he explained.

I thought that I would put him down, but he parried my blow with ease.

"Now I thrust, you parry", he said. "Concentrate, it not easy."

I nodded and said something like "yes, yes". Bradakos executed the straight thrust, I parried, but it had no effect and I ended up on my arse.

"You parry like little girl", he said.

I scowled in reply.

By the end of the following month I could breach his defences maybe once every lesson, and he only put me on my arse about a dozen times during the same time span. I couldn't help feeling like a failure. I imagined being this great natural warrior, but compared to the king's champion I was nothing.

One day, not long after, I noticed Nik watching while we trained with the spear. That evening he said, "Lucius, I can see that you are discouraged. But remember who you are training with. That man fights like a god in battle. He is brutally strong, lightning fast, and no fool. You are a boy. I saw you practise today. I couldn't believe that you hit him once or twice with the shaft. I don't believe that there is any man in this camp who can get through his defences like you did. Not even me, and I am no fool with a spear."

Maybe it was something Nik said, maybe it was because I was coming of age, but something happened inside me. I wanted to be able to beat Bradakos. The gods intervened and gave me patience because by this time I understood that only training could help me and not desire alone.

Chapter 12 – Warrior

Nik was an educated man, but a warrior at heart. That was the only reason I was able to persuade him to help me with the weapons training and let the bookwork slip a little. Just a little, though.

Every evening, the hour before sunset, Nik stood by as I practised my moves against a dead tree trunk close to the river. He mostly watched - sometimes correcting my feet, or maybe altering my strike angle.

I did not tell Bradakos about this.

Two moons passed and we were training with spear shafts, when Bradakos simply took a step back and threw his on the ground. "You fight like man now. Tomorrow I bring sword." That was all, but coming from him, I couldn't have been given a bigger compliment.

I was excited about the upcoming training. Nik was a master of the sword in his own right, and had trained me with a wooden weapon since I was strong enough to wield it.

Early the following morning I was on the training field, waiting impatiently for Bradakos. He eventually arrived, carrying two metal swords. Not wooden swords as I had expected.

"Nik tell me you know sword. We see", he said, and handed me one. I tested the weapon for weight and balance. It felt good. I also noticed that it was blunted, and sighed with relief.

He came at me, lightning fast. Just to put it into perspective, I was no master swordsman then, but I knew the basics, and I knew it well.

I parried his thrusts, his overhead strikes and his blows to my legs. He was so fast, I didn't even think of a counter attack.

"Nik show you defence. He show you how to attack?" Bradakos asked. I nodded, he answered with a nod, and I had a go at him. I was still a boy, but the training of the past months had made me strong and fast.

I think if we had met on the battlefield, he would have killed me almost instantly, but he had to be reserved, testing me without hurting me. I initiated the attack by lunging forward with my right leg. I drew back the weapon over my shoulder and slashed from left to right, aiming at his face. He parried as I would have expected of a professional, with a simple frontal parry. As our swords met, I turned my hand over and angled a thrust around his sword, my left hand gripping his right arm. But he surprised me by freeing his arm and grabbing the blade.

We both froze for a second. Then he smiled, the first time in nearly a year.

He stepped back and nodded. "That is good, but I not dead yet," he said slyly.

We stopped fencing and he showed me thrusts, parries and drills. I was familiar with most, but I enjoyed the slight differences. That evening during my training with Nik, I showed him what I had been taught, and we discussed the drawbacks and benefits. I was learning, changing - I was becoming a warrior.

The next morning, Bradakos was waiting for me with a chain mail shirt in his hand. Chain mail is very hard to come by in the world of the Scythians and I nodded appreciatively.

He assisted me in fitting the mail shirt. "Only take off for sleeping and washing. Now we run."

Running with chain mail is a different kettle of fish than running without it. We ran the same distance as always. At least I didn't vomit, but came close. I had three bowls of the meat stew and two mugs of goat milk.

I did as I was told. I removed the mail only when absolutely necessary. At first it hurt me terribly, but Nik arranged for a padded undergarment of felt, worn over my tunic and underneath the mail, which stopped the chafing. Within weeks I became used to wearing the mail, and didn't even notice it anymore. My body was adapting and growing stronger.

My next progression was weapons training while mounted. Nik had taught me how to wield a bow from the back of a horse, but my training was only rudimentary. This was different, more relentless, uncompromising. Most days I came home with bleeding fingers from shooting the bow, as well as a multitude of very tender spots where Bradakos had hit me with some sort of weapon, and I loved it.

During my first years with the Roxolani I didn't see the king at all, apart from a glimpse in the distance. He wanted to keep our relationship and my possible succession a secret. Bradakos's mentorship of me might have sparked a couple of questions, but I am sure they fabricated a story. I trained six days of the week. On my day off I was usually so tired that I spent most of the day lying down or sitting next to the hearth fire, conversing with Nik, in Scythian, of course.

Chapter 13 – Migration

"The king has requested our presence. We are to dine with him in private this evening", Nik said, raising his eyebrows.

"It sounds very formal, Nik. Do you know what it is about?" I replied. "Am I in any kind of trouble?"

"Relax, Lucius. It's just a meal with a friend", Nik sighed.

By then, we had lived with the tribe for more than four years. I spoke Scythian fluently, I wore their clothes, and my hair was braided and tied at the back. My shoulders were broad and my chest and back muscular, a product of training with bow and sword. I was tall, lean and deceptively strong. I had just turned seventeen.

We dressed neatly in our best loose-fitting Scythian tunics with long sleeves. Nik was cleanly shaven. One habit he struggled to break, was shaving. I had no beard to speak of yet.

We strolled over to the tent of the king at the appointed hour, where Bradakos was waiting for us at the entrance. "Greetings, Nik. Greetings, Eochar", he said formally.

Oh yes, did I forget to mention that I had to adopt a Scythian name? I was now called Eochar. Nik still called me Lucius, though, but only in private.

Bradakos ushered us into the tent of the king and gestured for us to take seats on the rich furs beside the hearth.

A slave poured wine into golden cups while we waited for the king to arrive. Bradakos surprised me by initiating a conversation. It was really unlike him. I would have been less surprised if he had produced a sword and taken the head of the slave for some undefined infringement.

"Nik, the progress of Eochar is most satisfactory", my mentor said. "He is no novice anymore."

Well, that made me feel good, and slightly like a novice. He had the ability to do that. Bastard.

Before Bradakos could make further small talk, the king arrived. He was dressed simply. I would have liked to say that he looked kingly or majestic or something along those lines, but the only word to describe his appearance that evening was "tired".

Nik rose, embraced him, and said, "Apsikal, my king, you look tired. Relax this evening, you are among friends."

Apsikal smiled, patted Nik's back and said, "Thank you, old friend, but there are things that weigh heavily upon me. I am here to seek advice, and to ask for your help."

"The Goths are migrating from the northeast", Apsikal said. "They are hungry for land and plunder, and are as numerous as the stars in the sky. They are not yet upon us, but at this rate we could engage them in a year or two. The Roxolani cannot afford to face them alone in open battle, they are too many. We must either make peace and pay tribute, or call on our allies."

The way he said "allies" was not comforting.

"Apsikal, who are the allies you are referring to?" Nik ventured.

"Far to the east there is a tribe known as the Urugundi. We have fought alongside them to keep the people of the distant east from taking their lands. The Urugundi have many allies themselves, and we can call on them to fight by our side. The problem is, the eastern nomads are different from us. We have never asked them to come to our aid, as we have done for them in the past. Once they assist us, and get a glimpse of the lands to the west, they will covet it and return to take our enemies' lands for themselves."

"The Urugundi and their allies, or the Huns as we call them, are matched by our warriors man to man. But our friends the Huns are more dangerous than any of our enemies. They live in extreme conditions and they feel no mercy, neither do they give a quarter. They live off the land, enduring hardship and cold. They disfigure the heads of their babies from birth, and do not shy away from drinking blood and eating meat raw. We have honour. The Huns have only bloodlust."

"I am sure they would help us to defeat the enemy, but at what cost? It could cost us our children's future."

The king appeared reflective, and continued.

"Many years ago, when I was but a little boy, there was a man in our village who owned many sheep. He was very wealthy and continuously laboured to increase the size of his flock. Then came a time when we were plagued by wolves. More than usual. Maybe it was the weather, maybe their natural prey was less abundant, who knows. Due to these predators, he lost many sheep. He tried everything, but to no avail. One day he came home with a bear cub. He found it after its mother had died. He raised the cub by hand, and when it was older, he taught the bear to watch over his sheep. The bear kept the wolves away, and now and again even killed one or two. The whole tribe heard of what the man had done, and they were impressed. Then a message arrived, requesting the man to visit his flock. On his arrival he found that the bear had killed the shepherd and the sheep. The flock was in a corral, and the bear did not leave a single one alive. He killed for the pleasure of killing, not for food. The owner was so distraught that he attacked the bear with a spear, but the bear killed him as well."

"I think of this tale, and I can't help to feel like this man. Should I allow the Gothic wolves to kill my flock, or should I ask the bear to help me deal with the wolves?"

Nik exchanged glances with me and the king in turn. "Apsikal, allow Eochar and me to travel to the lands of the Urugundi. If you wish the ancient bonds to be bolstered, I suggest we strengthen them with blood. We could call it a year of fostering for your nephew. He will fight at their side and forge ties as strong as iron."

Apsikal looked at Bradakos and asked, "Bradakos, what are your thoughts on this?"

Bradakos scowled, his friendliest scowl, though, and replied, "My king. The Urugundi are a fearsome people. If Eochar wants to rule this tribe in years to come, he would need the respect of the warriors. It is easier to respect a man who is hard as iron. Send him northwest, but send me with, I volunteer."

Talk about a sudden change in the direction of your life. I enjoyed the hard training every day, and I felt at home with the Roxolani. They were my people, after all.

Chapter 14 – Traveller

"When you travel across the Sea of Grass", Bradakos explained, "you need to exercise care. Should your retinue be too small, random brigands might attack and kill you, if your retinue is too large, a local chieftain might decide that you are an invading force."

Nik, Bradakos and I set off with an escort of twelve warriors, carefully selected by Bradakos, of course. I knew most of them, and they were all hard, dangerous men. Each of us had a spare horse which also doubled as a pack animal.

We journeyed until we sighted the shore of the Dark Sea. Nik and I had never travelled this far to the east. Bradakos had. He told us that we would journey more or less due east, keeping the shore of the Dark Sea on our right, and eventually reach the marshland of the Maeotis Swamp. We would skirt the swamp area and cross the river Don. The next major river to be crossed would be the Volga, then the Ural. Somewhere, east of the Ural, we would find the nomads we were seeking.

The first weeks of our journey were uneventful for the most part. We passed through breathtaking countryside and for the first time I understood why the people called it the Sea of Grass. Unending grasslands, stretching as far as the eye can see, to every horizon. This continued for days, creating the impression that it is endless. We passed through spectacular river valleys and stood on the shores of the bluest lakes with a backdrop of snow-capped mountains in the distance.

After a couple of weeks, one starts to relax, which can be problematic. Thanks to Bradakos's guidance, we largely avoided the warriors of the tribal lands that we traversed. His guides ranged far ahead of us to ensure that we stayed clear of danger.

We did once run into a patrol of the Alani, a tribe related to the Roxolani. Bradakos rode out to meet them, they accepted us as friends, and escorted us across their tribal lands.

Even though we didn't expect a fight, we donned our full armour every day, and rode with our bows strung. I still used the Roman shortsword that Nik took off the assassin. It was beautifully made, strong and flexible, with hardened cutting edges welded onto the blade. A fine weapon.

My bow was a present from my uncle, the king. A recurve bow that took five years to construct, made by the craftsmen employed by the king. Accurate, beautiful and powerful beyond belief.

Strapped to my saddle was a spear with a thick shaft, a practical battle axe, two full quivers and a couple of javelins. To summarise, we were well armed.

One of the scouts ranged ahead and one trailed a mile behind. Better to be safe than sorry.

I recall that we were discussing the benefits of a barbed arrow versus an armour-piercing arrow when the advance scout appeared, permeated with dust, his horse lathered. He reined in and reported to Bradakos, "Ten men on horses chasing one, they look like brigands. No armour, but they have spears and three of them have bows. Two miles ahead."

Bradakos smiled. I think the idea of shedding blood excited him. "Let's go save a traveller", he yelled, raised his arm in the air, and galloped off with all of us in tow.

As we neared the crest of a ridge, I dropped my reins, steered my galloping horse with my knees and nocked an arrow to my bow, with three more in my draw hand. I led the group, with Bradakos to my left. I took in the scene in front of me. One man, the traveller, stood dismounted with his back to a rocky outcrop. Five dead bandits lay at his feet. He was holding a longsword in a two-handed grip, obviously in a guard position. From his shoulder protruded an arrow, and his robes were stained red with blood. Two men with arrows nocked approached him, with a third ready to throw a spear.

I led the charge and acted without thinking, my arrow skewering the neck of the closest bandit. As I released my second arrow, the remaining bandit released his. Then I witnessed something that I have never dreamt possible. The swordsman struck the arrow mid-air with his sword. My second arrow ended the life of the second archer. Using his heavy spear, Bradakos ran the third brigand through with such force that the victim was lifted off the ground.

I dismounted and cautiously walked over to the swordsman. He sheathed his sword, looked at me with his slanted eyes and said, "I owe you life, Scythian", and collapsed.

I turned around. Bradakos was still grinning. "Next time leave two for me. Respect your teacher", he said.

We decided to set up camp next to the road, to enable us to treat the wounded traveller. Bradakos commanded his men to bury the dead in a shallow grave and stack rocks on top. Not that he was a compassionate man, but corpses would attract vultures and give away our position to a possible foe.

After we set up camp, Nik had the traveller laid down inside a tent.

The arrow had passed straight through the soft tissue of his shoulder without hitting bone. "We need to remove the arrow", Nik said. "He is fortunate, the arrow did not pierce his lung."

The man was lying on his side, still unconscious, and moaning softly.

"Bradakos, hold him down while Lucius and I remove the arrow", Nik said.

Nik broke the shaft of the arrow as close to the entry point as possible and proceeded to rub the protruding shaft with vinegar and honey. He took a cloth, gripped the arrowhead and as much of the shaft as he could manage, and pulled with all his strength. For a moment I thought that he would not get it out, but the arrow suddenly came free, accompanied by a wet, sucking sound. Blood started to flow from the wound on both sides. He pressed a cloth, wetted in vinegar, on both wounds and said, "Lucius, see if there is some of the cloth of the cloak missing, or if the arrow only punctured it."

I fumbled with the garment, and to my dread realised that it was not intact. "Nik, there is a piece missing", I confirmed.

Nik frowned while retrieving a small metal forceps from his kit. He rinsed it with vinegar and probed the wound. I had to look away.

"I'd rather slit ten throats than watch this", Bradakos mumbled.

After a while Nik held up a piece of bloody cloth in triumph, "Got it!"

He placed honey and salve made from Scythian herbs on the wound, and bound it tightly. "Now it is in the hands of the gods. I have done all that I can."

Bradakos stood, and as he exited the tent, said, "We will camp here tonight. It will be time enough for this man to recover, or die."

I lifted the traveller's head, and Nik mixed a spoon of some concoction or other into a goblet of wine, which we slowly fed to the patient. "It is made from poppy flowers and will help him sleep tonight."

Nik then walked over to the warriors and exchanged words with them. Early evening they returned with wild fowl and herbs which they left outside the entrance to our tent.

"Lucius, I have a feeling that we should help this man", Nik said. "Don't ask me why, I just know. Gather wood or dried dung, start a fire, and help me to prepare a broth."

Later on, we slowly fed as much broth as possible to the wounded man. He kept most of it down.

That evening he slept between Nik and me in the small tent, while we took turns to watch over him.

Nik stared down at him and said, "This man is from the land of silk, a place the Romans call 'Serica'. Never before have I laid eyes on a man with slanted eyes. I have read that these

Easterners call Rome "Da Qin", the great land to the west. I pray that he will recover, as I would like to speak with him of his homeland."

Unsurprisingly we woke up tired. I was fortunate enough to discover glowing coals underneath the ash of the previous evening's fire. A short while later the wild fowl broth was warming over the blazing fire.

Nik emerged from the tent just as Bradakos arrived. He was leading his horse and looked ready to ride. Nik greeted him, took him by the arm, and led him twenty paces away.

While Bradakos was the de facto leader of our group, he had immense respect for Nik. They spoke softly. I saw Nik gesturing. Bradakos scowled and shook his head. He walked past me, and said without slowing down or making eye contact, "Bring your sword, we train hard today."

I sighed, strapped on my sword and started to count the bruises.

Chapter 15 – Recovery

I arrived back at the tent after a full watch of training with Bradakos, cursing Nik under my breath. Bradakos had a petty side, which is unusual for such a great warrior. He took his frustration with Nik out on me, although I managed to breach his defences a couple of times as well.

I ducked to enter the tent. To my surprise, our patient was awake and sitting upright, supported by Nik's leather saddle. Nik gestured for me to approach and said in Scythian, "Welcome Lucius, please meet Cai Lun."

Cai Lun bowed his head in the eastern way, and said in broken Scythian, "Good meet you, Lucius of the Da Qin."

I nodded in response.

The Scythian tribes are generally very hospitable towards lone travellers. If you are not at war with them or involved in a blood feud, you are safe as a traveller. It is considered rude to ask a traveller his business, or the reasons for his journey. So it was with Cai Lun. We would not ask questions, but wait until he volunteered information.

Nik looked at Cai Lun, but addressed me, "Our new friend requests to join us on our journey. Cai Lun feels obligated to us. In his culture, when you save someone's life, a great debt is owed to that person. He owes that debt to you, Lucius, and wishes to repay it by serving you in some way. He is honour bound to do it."

Cai Lun stared at me with a blank expression on his face. The men from Serica are renowned for this, I would discover.

His Scythian was passable, but he spoke in an odd way. "Lucius of the Da Qin, I teach you breathe. It only take year or two."

Well, I was obviously at a loss for words. I didn't have the heart to tell him that I knew how to breathe already. The stupidity of youth.

In any event, Cai Lun, or Cai as we came to call him, recovered quickly. He had a multitude of herbs and potions that he administered to his wound, and it healed within a remarkably short time. Even Bradakos showed surprise. Which in itself was surprising.

Chapter 16 – The Huns

Nothing can prepare you for meeting the Huns for the first time. In later years I heard the Huns mentioned in the same breath as the Roxolani. That can only be expected of someone who had never seen a Hun.

Two days after fording the Ural, Bradakos called a halt. We rested on the crest of a hill, below us an unending plain of grassland. He pointed down the hill and grinned, "We are now in the tribal lands of the Huns. When we meet them, do not touch your weapons - not your bow, nor the hilt of your sword. Nothing! Allow me to speak with them. I have visited here before."

I should have read more into Bradakos's grin. He rarely grinned.

Bradakos explained that it was the area of the Huns' summer camp and that we could expect to encounter some patrolling force or other.

A quarter of a watch had passed when we heard the unmistakable sound of a group of horsemen approaching. A span of heartbeats later, Bradakos reined in his horse and raised an open palm. Our group immediately came to a halt. The thundering sound of hooves increased in volume, but abruptly died away as the barbarians encircled us. As if by magic, horsemen appeared from the tall grass. There must have been at least seventy of them.

I studied them intently, yet tried not to make any kind of aggressive eye contact. It is common knowledge that trying to stare down a barbarian is not good for one's health. In most cases it would be considered a challenge to engage in single combat.

The horses of the Huns were small, even for ponies. They possessed huge curved heads with scruffy manes, hanging down to below the knees. Although small, they appeared calm and purposeful, radiating power and robustness.

The horses were pale in comparison to their riders. They were strong men, big and broad, who sat in the saddle as if they were one with the horse. Like they belonged there. They lacked the eastern look, yet their eyes were small, slightly slanted and deep set, giving the impression that they stared at you from deep inside their skulls. The front half of their heads were tattooed, scarred and shaven. The backs of their skulls were covered with thick, black hair fashioned into single, long braids, tied at regular intervals with leather or silver bindings. Their skulls were strangely elongated, which gave them a demon-like appearance. Their noses were small and deformed to facilitate the conical iron helmets that hung from their leather saddles.

They grew no beards and most had tattoos and scars on their cheeks.

These people may have been barbarians, but they wore the best of armour. All wore scale armour shirts. Some made of iron, and others of bone or horn. Their forearms were encased in boiled leather vambraces with sewn-in bone or iron strips for extra protection.

Their stocky legs were wrapped in deer hides, and they wore soft leather boots on their feet.

They bristled with weapons. The Hun warriors each carried a composite bow, slung over the shoulder, and an hourglass quiver tied to either side of the saddle. In addition to the bow, they were armed with longswords, medium spears with enormous iron heads, light javelins, and woven lasso ropes.

It was clear that these Huns were born and bred to be warriors. But there was something else that I noticed. Something that added to their war-like image and chilled me to the bone.

They carried trophies.

Some quivers were covered with the whitest of leather, made from the severed arms of enemies, the shrunken fingers visible and intact. The soft-worked scalps of vanquished warriors adorned many parts of their person. Some decorated saddles while others were stitched together to form a cloak.

Many warriors proudly displayed freshly taken scalps that were tied to their packs, dried blood staining the flanks of their horses.

The leader of the band walked his horse in our direction and stopped thirty paces from Bradakos. He held a spear in his hand, the muscles thick and ropey on his forearm, and his biceps crisscrossed with veins and scars from countless battles. He threw his spear at Bradakos, who slapped it from the air with his leather-covered wicker shield, and promptly dismounted. The Hun jumped off his horse with the grace of a cat and walked purposefully towards Bradakos. Both drew their swords. I was overcome by a feeling of dread as they closed with each other. The Hun advanced and rammed his sword into the soil in front of Bradakos, who did the same. Then the Hun grabbed our friend in a bear hug and lifted him off his feet while the other Hun warriors howled like wolves.

It took a while for my nerves to settle.

Bradakos walked over to us and said, "The Hun leader is called Octar. He is the king of the Huns. I have known him since we were young warriors. Follow us to their camp. I will introduce you later."

Bradakos and Octar vaulted onto their horses and raced off at breakneck speed, with the Hun horde following, and unsurprisingly, howling like wolves.

We made our way to the Hun camp with the rest of the warriors and the packhorses in tow, arriving by mid-afternoon.

I didn't know what to expect, but I was impressed. There were at least three thousand tents in the settlement, although it was difficult to be certain. The dwellings were arranged in distinct clusters. Although the groups were in close proximity to each other, they were separated by at least twenty paces. It was an indication of the factionalism within the grouping of Hun tribes. Huge circular tents, at least thirty paces in diameter, and mounted on wagons, were visible within each cluster. I assumed that those belonged to the nobles or leaders of the different clans. A variety of smaller tents were erected on the ground, or on the back of custom made two- and four-wheeled carts. All the tents seemed to be round or oval, and made of thick felt, fitted over a carcass of wood. Each dwelling had a hole in the centre of the roof to allow the smoke from the hearth fire to escape. The thick felt doors were richly painted or embroidered with vines, leaves or other scenes from nature.

Bradakos was waiting for us one hundred paces outside the tented village. His Hun friends seemed to have disappeared to attend to whatever Huns do.

"We must wait here", he said. "The king is arranging accommodation. We are fortunate. He still regards me as a friend, even though he is now a powerful man. We are invited to feast with Octar tonight."

While we were talking, tented wagons, drawn by oxen, arrived. They parked near the pavilion of the king.

"You will notice that all the felt doors face south. The Huns have great respect for the sun that dwells in the southern part of the sky, and believe it to be good fortune to allow the sunshine into their homes", Bradakos explained.

Before nightfall, slaves set up our accommodation, took care of our horses and even lit the central hearth fire common to every kind of tent. I started to warm to the Huns.

As soon as we had unpacked our belongings and donned clean tunics, we were summoned to attend the king. Our weapons and armour remained in our tents and were oiled, sharpened and polished by slaves.

The Roxolani warriors who escorted us were not invited to the king's feast, but two sheep were spitted next to our lodgings to feed them.

Nik, Cai, Bradakos and I walked over to the king's tent as soon as darkness descended. A set of steps led up to the wooden platform on which the tent was mounted. At the top, on either side of the big felt door, stood two Hun guards in full armour. Bradakos spoke to them in the tongue of the Huns. One of the guards nodded, ducked into the tent, and re-appeared moments later. He ushered us in.

The tent was enormous. Much larger than it appeared from the outside. Inside, everything was neatly organised. Thick, dark-coloured woollen carpets covered the floor while hanging carpets provided privacy to the sleeping area. In the middle of the room was the standard hearth, just a larger version fit for a king. One wall accommodated leather storage bags, while the other held household utensils, neatly stacked on racks. The king sat at the far side of the fire. Bradakos and I were ushered to the seats on his right, the place of honour. Nik and Cai sat on our right, opposite the king, the place reserved for male visitors. The slaves and servants took their expected places close to the felt door.

The king raised his hand, and a pouring slave filled our cups with warm sheep's milk mixed with honey. It tasted good, and dispelled the chill of the evening.

Octar and Bradakos conversed in the Hunnic language while the rest of us were sipping milk. Their tongue was similar to Scythian in many ways, but required some time getting used to. I was only able to understand a couple of words.

Octar surprised me then by speaking in perfect Scythian. He spoke louder, clearly meant for all of us, and not just for Bradakos. "The Huns welcome the envoy from the Roxolani. Our people have been allies for generations. Although we are different, we are all people of the Sea of Grass and we will stand together against our common enemies."

"Thank you for your words, high king of the Huns", Bradakos said. "I, for one, know you as a man of honour, and the purpose of our visit is to strengthen the bond of friendship between our people."

When the initial formalities had been taken care of, Octar seemed to relax and he continued, looking at Bradakos, "How can the Huns help their friends?"

Bradakos took a long gulp of the sweet milk, scowled, and said, "Have you heard of a race called the Goths? They are said to come from the lands of the Ice Islands, across the large water of the north. They are a dirty race that toils the earth, and sometimes stay in the same place for years. They do not understand the way of the horse or the bow, but they try to be like us. Goths are big men, fierce, but without the skill of the Scythians. They are numerous, more numerous than the Roxolani. They will swallow us, and once they have spit us out, they will subdue the other tribes one by one."

"The threat is not immediate, but our people need to strengthen our tribal bonds. We foresee that a time will come when the Hun and the Roxolani fight side by side to rid the Sea of Grass of these dirty people."

Octar listened, but said nothing. It was their way. You do not interrupt a man until he has made it clear that he has finished speaking.

Bradakos remained silent for thirty heartbeats and then continued. "The young warrior to my left is called Eochar - the nephew and heir of the Roxolani king. It is the wish of our king for Eochar to learn the ways of the Hun warrior and stay with your people to strengthen our bond."

Octar again remained silent until he was certain that Bradakos had said all he wanted to say. He did not reply to Bradakos's words, as it was not expected. The king would decide, and summon us when he so desires.

"Bradakos, my friend, please introduce our other guests", Octar said.

Bradakos gestured to Nik and said, "Nik is an old friend of mine. He is a Roman, from the Empire to the west. He is also the father of Eochar. Nik is a famous warrior among the Romans. Do not be fooled by his grey hair."

Octar smiled and said, "Nik of the Romans, welcome to my lands. A friend of Bradakos is a friend of mine. I cannot wait to see your skills with the sword. The fame of your people is well known in these lands. One day I would like to test the skill of the Huns against the might of the legions of Rome."

Bradakos waited a couple of heartbeats until he was sure that the king had finished. "On our way to you we rescued an honourable traveller from bandits. He is from the land of Serica."

Cai inclined his head to show his respect.

Octar stared intently at Cai. "You are welcome in my lands, man from Serica. Make no mistake, if you are a spy of the eastern raiders, I will deal with you harshly."

Cai turned to Bradakos and asked, "May I address king?"

Bradakos looked at Octar, who nodded. "Great king of Huns, my people live far to east, beyond territory of eastern nomads. I no friend to these people. I am on quest to land of the Da Qin and I owe Eochar life. Please allow me teach him and remain in land of Hun."

Octar nodded. He had heard Cai's request and would consider it.

The king lifted his cup, and a slave rushed over and filled it to the brim. "We have disposed with the formalities, let us feast and talk about old times."

Chapter 17 – Leaving camp

The Huns do not cultivate grapes or produce wine. Wine was an oddity, even at the table of the king. We were served a sweet-tasting liquid made from honey. Bradakos told me that it is called mead. He however failed to tell me about the effects of overindulging. Typical.

I woke early in the morning with the worst headache I have ever experienced.

As I crawled out of my tent, Bradakos strolled over, obviously looking as fresh as a daisy. "Come, we have to train", he said, and smiled.

I had trouble walking, but indulged the mean bastard, donned my mail, collected my weapons and followed him.

We ran, but were forced to stop almost every mile to allow me to vomit. We sparred, but had to stop frequently so I could at least try to vomit. I think I might have passed out once or twice as well. Nonetheless, I managed to get through the day somehow. After training I was allowed to recover in my tent for the rest of the day. Nik and Cai were well aware of my ailment, and by late morning Cai entered my tent with an unknown potion mixed with water.

"Eochar of the Da Qin, you have much more learn", Cai said. "Remember, first man takes drink, then drink takes man."

Try to make sense of philosophy when you feel like dying. I swallowed the potion, nearly vomited, and fell asleep. I awoke late afternoon feeling right as rain.

Bradakos, Nik and Cai were sitting outside when I skulked out of the tent. Bradakos scowled and said, "Good news, my young friend. The king has agreed to our request, meaning that you may stay with the Huns for a year. Nik, Cai and I will also stay."

"The king also mentioned that they will teach you to behave properly at a feast", he added.

I didn't know if Bradakos was jesting. I couldn't remember anything I did or said after the third cup of mead. Sometimes it is wiser not to offer a response.

Bradakos continued. "There are, however, certain conditions that the king insists on. Nik and I will not stay with you. You will live with the warriors. Cai will be allowed to train you every day, and when you travel, Cai will be the one to accompany you - obviously to allow him to continue your training. Nik and I will be in camp, and you may visit us from time to time."

I didn't realise it then, but Octar wanted me to learn to be my own man, but he needed someone to look after me while on campaign. It would have been a diplomatic fiasco if I died while living with the Huns. In any event, it was given to me as a fait accompli, so I just nodded and smiled.

Bradakos added, "Tomorrow morning a band of warriors is leaving to patrol the eastern borders. There have been minor incursions into the lands of the Huns. The king is sending three hundred warriors to investigate. You and Cai will join them."

Again, I nodded and smiled.

That evening I said goodbye to Nik and Bradakos. We sat with Cai around the hearth of our tent and sipped hot milk.

For the first time, Cai spoke about himself. "To east, there is great empire. It called Empire of Han. I hear Nik say Romans speak of Serica. It not unlike your Rome. The Empire of Serica attacked from outside by barbarian tribes. Wild men are defeated, time and again. Then more appear from endless lands to north and west. From inside, Empire threatened by internal strife. This is fruit of greed."

Nik looked at Cai, sighed and said, "Cai, it sounds similar to what is happening with Rome. Rome has defeated the fierce Germanic tribes during the long Marcomanni invasions, but there will always be new enemies - barbarians who covet the wealth of civilisation. Like in Serica, greed and the lust for power are destroying the Empire from within."

Cai looked at Nik, smiled sadly, and said, "Even though empires thousand miles apart, I believe that what happen in my land influence yours. Bradakos tells that tomorrow we investigate incursions into land of Huns. My people recently defeat ancient and terrible enemy, the Xiong-nu - barbarian horse warriors of north. They now weak, and they forced to flee west. The Xianbei, even worse barbarian tribe, nipping at their heels. I not surprised if sudden incursion is sign of what is to come. World wishes to be in balance. It need be restored to great Empire of West and Great Empire of East. Only then will we hold at bay barbarians. If this not happen, long period of darkness descend over both our lands. It take hundreds of years to undo."

Cai turned his gaze to me and said, "Lucius of the Da Qin, I travel with you tomorrow, and make no mistake, we travel to war." He rose, walked over to his tent, and emerged a few heartbeats later, carrying a linen bag. He sat down again and opened the bag. Inside was a meticulously folded garment of a bright yellow colour. My initial impression was that it was some kind of dress worn to a feast.

"Lucius of the Da Qin, you wear this under armour tomorrow", Cai said.

I extended my hand to inspect the ridiculous tunic. It was made of silk. Nik and Bradakos looked on with interest, especially Bradakos.

Nik felt the material and said, "It is certainly silk, but it is much thicker. What is this, Cai?"

"Nik, this garment made of silk. Vulnerable parts of body and upper arms protected by these", Cai said, and pointed to the stitched inlays. "Many layer of silk glued together. This shirt stop arrow better than scale shirt of iron."

Now he had the full and undivided attention of Bradakos, who wore the expression of a five-year-old tasting honey for the first time.

Cai cast Bradakos a sideways glance and smiled. "No need worry Bradakos, I have one for you as well," as he pulled another garment from the linen bag.

Nik supported Cai's claims. "Bradakos, I can see you are not convinced. I have seen this stop an arrow at short range. Even if the arrow does penetrate, the head of the arrow entangles itself in the fine silk thread and it is easy to remove."

Bradakos stared at the shirt with reverence, while feeling and stroking the material.

"Thank you for this gift, Cai", he said. "I place no value on treasure or gold, but this is the most excellent gift that I have ever received."

Well, at least it would keep Bradakos entertained for the next month. I'm sure he even slept in it that evening.

I stood, bowed to Cai in the eastern way, and said, "Thank you for your generous gift, Cai of the Han, I will heed your counsel and wear this tomorrow."

Chapter 18 – Rude awakening

Cai and I were ready the following morning before first light. I decided to err on the side of caution and wore the yellow silk undergarment beneath the scale armour made of horse hooves. I also donned my open face helmet. My extremities were protected by greaves and vambraces. With the addition of the bright yellow undergarment, my appearance resembled that of a court jester rather than a warrior. My suspicions were later confirmed by the mocking glances I received throughout the day.

Cai wore his yellow silk tunic beneath his scale armour. The scales looked to be made of linen, but Cai would elaborate when he wished to. We each had a pack with all the essentials and weapons. The only weapon Cai took was his sword.

Bradakos arrived just after sunrise with eight horses in tow. "These are your horses for the journey. They are from the king's herd", he explained.

It was clear that they were Hun horses, and he added, "Your own horses will not cope with this trip, these will get you there and back."

I must have said something like "sure". A typical reply for one my age.

Bradakos smiled and said, "You will see." His smile immediately eroded my confidence, replacing it with a nagging concern.

Bradakos led us to the edge of the camp where the warriors were assembling. He walked over to a fierce-looking Hun. He was of the same age as the Roxolani champion, and it seemed that they knew one another.

"Eochar", Bradakos said, "this warrior is called Gordas. He is a general in the Hun army. Show him the necessary respect, and please make an effort to understand the Hun language. I have asked him to talk slowly when he speaks to you. The king has explained the situation to him, and you and Cai will travel as part of the group. But remember, there will be no special treatment. You will be treated as a Hun."

I inclined my head to Gordas, who said nothing, and scowled. With that, Bradakos slapped my horse's rump and our group of warriors left at a gallop.

The pace they set was nothing short of brutal. We changed horses four times every watch at the signal of the general. Let me explain how the Huns go about it. The least able of their riders slow the horse down to a walk, jump off, and vault onto the next horse. They do not use saddles when they cover great distances, because they have to change horses regularly. The better riders display their skill by jumping from one horse to the next at nearly full gallop.

Bradakos had a kind side to him as well. All our spare horses were saddled. We just stopped, jumped off, remounted, and rode on. After about two watches of riding hard, I was exhausted. We had travelled nearly fifty miles. My waterskin was empty, my legs were burning like fire, and my arse was worn through to the bone. I was close to giving up. I could see that Cai was struggling, but he wore the mask of the Easterners, and showed no emotion.

What do you do when you can't go on, but giving up is not an option?

I didn't expect my first lesson in the gentle art of breathing. Cai rode beside me and said, "I will help you to make it. Breathe deep and slow, through nose. Breathe into belly. Imagine you are in mother's womb, breathing through navel. Use muscles in stomach to breathe."

It sounded like nonsense to me, but I was desperate and close to falling off my horse, so I tried. I did more than try. I put my heart and soul into it. I thought about nothing else but breathing. Something happened then. It is difficult to explain, but after a while I was not hurting anymore, I was removed from the pain and somehow relaxed.

Cai told me to rest my tongue lightly against the roof of my mouth. My thirst disappeared as my mouth produced more saliva. Weird. I kept up with the breathing.

We rode eighty miles that day. I did not think it possible. As soon as I dismounted, I collapsed. The Huns around me looked only mildly tired. They stared at me in obvious disgust. The soft boy who knows the king. I could see it in their eyes.

To my shame I must admit that Cai erected our tent that evening, and cooked the food. I just lay in the tent, unable to move. He even fetched water for me. I felt like a failure.

On the morrow, Cai woke me from a dreamless sleep, fed me hot porridge mixed with meat and milk, and helped me into the saddle. We rode again.

The terrain was generally flat, as the Sea of Grass tends to be. I soon suspected that the distance travelled during the previous day was not unusual for the Huns. At this realisation, my initial reaction was panic, which was soon replaced by a calm acceptance of my lot when I started breathing in the eastern way. It carried me through the day. Just.

Unsurprisingly I collapsed again. Cai did everything, the Huns looked at me funny, and I slept. Deeply.

Cai fed me, helped me into the saddle. We rode. I panicked. Breathed. Just made it. Same story.

I think I was hovering somewhere between life and death, but I made it. No thanks to myself, but thanks to Cai's efforts.

We rested on the sixth day. We had come five hundred miles, and the horses needed rest. Gordas called a halt beside a stream surrounded with green pastures. Each man had four horses, so we had more than a thousand horses to feed.

The seventh day we rode again and I coped. I was well fed, rested and breathing, and I enjoyed it.

Believe it or not, it was possible for me to have a conversation with Cai the evening before we went to bed.

Cai told me that he was a priest of the Dao religion. The religion is unlike the Roman or Scythian religions where gods are worshipped. Daoism aims to strengthen and balance the life force in the body to achieve immortality. This is done through meditation, breathing and physical training.

To train with the sword, or jian, as Cai called it, is a way to achieve a higher spiritual plane, the Dao.

By perfecting his skill, his mind is also elevated. Needless to say, I didn't understand any of it.

For years he lived in a valley called Hanzhong, but their peace was torn apart by internal strife in the empire, and he had to flee.

I slept well that evening and woke up refreshed. Eager for the challenge of the day.

Gordas summoned all the warriors and issued instructions. I followed little of what he said. When the warriors dispersed to their horses, Gordas signalled for me to attend him. I walked over to the Hun. Although he spoke for long, I only understood a few words. "Today we reach borderland. Weapons sharp. No stupid. Try not ride like girl and stay on horse."

I nodded in shame and understanding, and walked away.

I told Cai that we would be reaching our destination that day. I left out the part about the girl.

Cai spoke while fiddling with his horse's tack, his back turned to me. "I have feeling today Huns will meet Xiong-nu", he said. "I hope they not underestimate them. Xiong-nu sly and ferocious race."

Gordas set a relaxed pace. I believe that he did not want to risk engaging the enemy on blown horses.

We were close to the crest of one of the rolling hills when Gordas held up his hand. One of the outriders came galloping up to him to report. It was obvious that he had ridden hard and had important information for the general.

Gordas listened to the words of the scout and shouted, "Leave spare horses."

Five warriors, who did not look happy, dismounted and rounded up the spare horses. Gordas had obviously detailed them to stay with that purpose in mind.

I noticed the other warriors stringing their bows and fiddling with their weapons. I followed suit. Cai and I rode near the rear of the column, as was expected.

The band advanced on Gordas's signal. As we crested the hill, I took in the scene. Before us lay a sprawling valley, or rather, an area surrounded by two of the gentle rolling hills so typical of this landscape. A tented camp, or settlement of some kind, lay to the west of the valley floor. It was not large, maybe twenty tents at the most. A contingent of horse warriors were attacking the settlement. The group was not as numerous as our band, but still consisted of at least two hundred warriors.

Cai pointed to the right and said, "Look at crest of hill. Quick!"

Then I saw it, the faint glint of metal in the sunlight. It was only there for a fleeting moment, and then gone.

The Huns charged at breakneck speed. They were keen to close with the enemy, who was about eight hundred paces distant. Cai and I were right there with them, keeping up. The

Huns howled like wolves, their muscles bulging, eager for the kill.

I steered my horse with my knees, an arrow nocked, and a couple more in my draw hand. Without warning, my horse collapsed from underneath me. Even at my age I was a skilled rider, and I rolled as I hit the ground. The soil was soft and absorbed most of the impact. My body was intact, but my pride was utterly destroyed.

I saw Cai rein in, turn his horse around and trot back in my direction. My horse's leg was broken, the bone protruding from the wound. I took my sword from the saddlebag, stroked his head, and sent him away on his final journey. It's always hard to kill a wounded animal. I have no such issues concerning men.

Cai soon reached me and dismounted. The hill provided an excellent vantage point from which to view the battle. The Easterner pointed at the Hun horsemen. "We watch", he said.

When charging, the Huns seem to be an unorganized rabble. That is an illusion. When they are ready to engage, they deploy in a variety of ways. The leader issues a yelp or similar signal which they are familiar with, and they immediately react to the command.

As the milling mass of horsemen approached the Xiong-nu riders, they widened their front and split into at least ten wedge formations. The enemy riders bunched together in detached groups, clearly surprised at the sudden arrival of the Huns. Two hundred paces from the enemy, the Huns released their first arrows.

Hun warriors are able to shoot an arrow every heartbeat. Thousands of arrows struck the confused enemy, and predictably, they broke. Or so it seemed. Half of the insurgents were annihilated in the first attack, and the survivors lay flat on their horses, fleeing for their lives. The Huns pursued at full gallop, continuously releasing arrows into the rear of the fleeing enemy.

Cai looked on, concern etched on his face. As the Xiong-nu warriors ascended the far hill, a dark line of horse warriors appeared on both sides of the surrounding crests. It was difficult to estimate their numbers, but there were at least two thousand. It was a trap. The enemy wings closed around the group of Huns and poured arrows into their ranks.

"Lucius, retrieve your weapons!" Cai yelled.

I grabbed my sword, bow and quiver, vaulted onto Cai's horse, and we rode away at a gallop. The Xiong-nu warriors were too occupied with the remaining Huns to pay us any notice.

We soon reached the five warriors who were left to guard the horses. I tried to explain to them the fate of their fellows.

Cai said to them in his best Scythian, "Go tell king of Huns what happen. Take horses. We cannot let enemy take them. Leave now, they will come. Leave twenty horses."

The Huns understood. They nodded, although they appeared reluctant. One, who seemed to be the leader, said, "We go, but we will have revenge. That is the way of the Hun."

Cai rounded up our pack animals while I randomly selected horses from the herd. The horse minders mounted and expertly herded the horses away at speed, displaying their unbelievable skills with the animals.

Cai and I found ourselves alone. With twenty Hun horses to keep us company.

Chapter 19 – Rescue

Cai seemed less concerned than me. "First, we need good place make camp."

I couldn't argue with that.

For nearly a watch we rode west, travelling along the same route we had used earlier in the day. Cai recalled a rocky outcrop that would provide us with more than adequate cover.

We stumbled upon a small cave when we explored the hillock. In one corner we discovered the remains of a campfire, but it was clear that no one had visited within the last few moons. Normally we would not light a fire so close to the enemy, but we found dry wood, and in addition the cave would shield the fire from possible enemy scouts. I ventured out to kill a couple of wild fowl for the evening meal.

On my return, we feasted on the birds even though our minds were elsewhere.

"Many of my people live among Xiong-nu", Cai said. "I speak language of barbarians."

I nodded and wondered where the conversation was going. I did not have to wait long.

"I go to Xiong-nu camp", he said. "Mayhap we rescue Huns. Surely not all of them dead."

I went cold on the inside. It sounded risky.

"Cai, I will go with you", I heard myself say.

Cai nodded.

The following day we slept late and ate the leftovers of the wild fowl for breakfast. We did not dare light a fire during the daytime. The rest of the day we spent at our hideout, planning.

At sunset we set out on our insane mission.

We rode to the ridge where, nearly two days before, we first laid eyes on the thousands of barbarian horsemen. Cai held up his hand, and we dismounted. We crested the hill on foot. It was a sight to behold. Thousands of campfires illuminated the landscape.

"You wait here, Lucius of the Da Qin. 1 go gather information. See to horses", he commanded.

Cai didn't wait for an answer, but started down the hill. The closest fires were a mile away. I did what I was told, and walked back to the horses.

Time seemed to stand still. I waited and waited, and imagined an enemy sentry in every shadow. I was sure that daylight would arrive at any moment and leave me exposed to the eager eyes of the invaders.

Eventually I heard Cai's voice call from the darkness. "I am here, Lucius of the Da Qin. Do not put arrow in me."

I let go of the nocked arrow and exhaled. "Do not be concerned, Cai of Serica, I knew it was you approaching", I lied.

Cai waved away my comment. "It is camp of Xiong-nu. Many of my people among them. They fled land of Han due to upheaval I told you about. I move about their camp without fear they notice me. Nobody expects man from land of Han to roam countryside."

Cai motioned for me to follow him and he mounted his horse. "I found Hun captives. Only five left alive. They keep Huns next to river, away from camp. Priest of Xiong-nu performing cleansing ceremony, to prepare them for sacrifice to Goytosir, their bloodthirsty god of sun and sky. Gordas also alive, but have bad wound."

We travelled in silence for the rest of the way to our hideout, each occupied with his own thoughts. We would have to decide whether to rescue the Huns or leave them to an unimaginable fate.

The sun appeared on the horizon as we arrived at our camp. We had no food, but we were dead tired and fell asleep almost immediately, only waking in the early afternoon.

Cai was sitting cross-legged on the ground not far from me, obviously in deep meditation. I decided to let him finish with whatever he was doing and occupied myself with my own thoughts. I had made up my mind. I would attempt to rescue Gordas and his men, with or without Cai. I was honour bound to try.

Cai descended from wherever he was and stared at me intently. "Lucius of the Da Qin, I can see that you make decision. We leave within half a watch."

With our minds made up, we needed a plan.

We would have to circle the Xiong-nu camp and approach from the direction of the river, which would add at least a third of a watch to our travelling time. We would need horses for the captives, and spares as well, if a chase ensued. The rest was uncertain.

We set off. At least we had a plan, if you could call it that.

The camp of the Xiong-nu was to the west of the river, but the captives were held on the eastern side. Only when they were cleansed by the shaman could they cross the river to make their final journey. That in itself was a blessing sent by the gods.

Should the prisoners have been held in the middle of the encampment, our shades would now be walking the lands of the east.

In any event, a full watch later, we were close to the enemy camp when our first problem arose. We crawled to the top of the hill bordering the camp. Peering over, we saw the watchmen. Five horse warriors were sitting beside a fire, conversing in raised voices. They were poor sentries. I was certain that liquor was involved as well. Even so, a blind man would be able to see our approach over the hill in daylight, so we had to wait.

We modified our plan, deciding that we would approach under cover of darkness. Cai would circle around the sentries to ensure that none escaped alive. A simple plan.

When the darkness was thick around us, we put our plan into action. Slowly and silently we made our way towards the sentries. A hundred paces from their campfire I kneeled down and nodded to Cai, who issued a curt grunt of acknowledgement and continued his advance. I waited patiently until I believed Cai was in position. There was no way to be sure, though.

When I could wait no longer, I took five arrows from my quiver. One I notched to the bow, three more I held in my draw hand, as I had been taught by Nik years before. Another

I planted in the soil in front of me. I inhaled deeply and then breathed slowly until I felt calm. This was an easy shot in daylight, at a stationary target, but in practice, ...?

I exhaled slowly and deliberately. My first arrow entered the back of the man facing away from me. The second pierced the heart of the man facing him. The third man went down with an arrow protruding from his temple. My fourth arrow missed the mark completely, but the arrow I pulled from the ground took the fifth man in the buttocks. They ran. The buttocks man ran slower and died last. Cai was in position and easily dispatched the two surviving sentries. I casually walked over to the fire. The sentries had been grilling cuts of beef over the open flames. Without thinking I took the food and placed it in a leather bag I poached off one of the dead men. He would no longer need it.

We retraced our steps and collected the horses, which took nearly a third of a watch. Then we rode in search of the tent of the shaman.

Cai called a halt. He pointed to a tent illuminated by a blazing fire. I reached for my bow, but Cai shook his head and pointed to my sword. We hobbled the horses, which took longer than we thought, and advanced towards the tent. The pavilion was easily thirty paces in diameter, which indicated that the shaman was revered in the Xiong-nu culture. There was no way to establish how many guards were inside, although none guarded the entrance.

Since there were no other options apart from entering the tent by force and killing all the enemies, we exchanged glances, nodded, and advanced.

We scouted around the tent to make sure there were no warriors in close proximity. There were none.

Cai and I walked to the felt door, swept the covering aside, and entered.

Inside we found the shaman and the five Hun prisoners, as well as ten of the enemy guards. My sword was already in my hand, but I was temporarily stunned. Ten against two were poor odds. Even I knew that.

I was a capable swordsman, having trained with Nik for ten years, and five with Bradakos, but no one could surmount these odds. I had never seen the skills of Cai, but I imagined it to be average at best.

How very wrong I was. As Cai stepped inside the tent, he drew his sword in one fluent motion. I think he killed three of the warriors before they were able to draw their weapons. It appeared as if he was performing some kind of dance ritual. Moves I had never seen before. As the enemy swordsmen engaged him, his weapon seemed to slide off their blades and end up in a killing stroke. It was enchanting to watch. And watch was all I did. Within heartbeats, all of the enemy were dead, or dying. Including the shaman.

I don't know who was more surprised, the Huns or me. Cai cut the bonds of the prisoners and said, "Come, Lucius of the Da Qin, time is our enemy."

Gordas had to be supported between two of his men due to the arrow wound to his leg. The burning sickness had set in and he was delirious.

The horses were close by, only a hundred paces away. Soon all of us were mounted. Gordas had to mount with one of his men, as he was too weak to ride on his own.

"We ride to camp. Fast. This man need my ministrations, else he die", Cai said with a look of concern.

We travelled at speed, changing horses at least three times, and reached camp with no visible pursuit.

While I lit a fire, Cai proceeded to clean Gordas's wound in the faint glow of the campfire. He removed the head of an arrow and applied his mix of herbs and honey, then bound it tightly. The Huns provided assistance in silence, but I saw in their eyes that they had a newfound respect for Cai.

We allowed Gordas to rest for an hour, then Cai said, "If we ride now, Gordas may die. If we stay, we already dead.

Xiong-nu pursue us until we captured. They not take slaying of shaman lightly."

Gordas's men expertly tied him to a horse. We rode like madmen, with the Huns as our guides. By daybreak we reached a minor river. We walked and led the horses downstream, with the flow of the river, to throw the enemy off our track.

The most senior man, besides Gordas, was a warrior named Tatos.

As Tatos exited the stream, he said, "We must rest while. For horses need take water." Nobody argued.

We lay down in the grass while Cai prepared a potion for Gordas, who looked to be close to death. I was drifting off to sleep when Tatos's voice pulled me back from the edge, "We ride, enemy will follow."

We rode.

At least I didn't need to worry about managing the ride intervals and watering the horses. Tatos and his men were experts. They knew the capabilities of their mounts and the location of the streams and rivers.

Chapter 20 – Pursuit

The remainder of the day passed without incident, although we rode for fear of our lives. Somehow it is easier to endure hardship when your life depends on it. You ponder less on the option of giving up, given the alternative.

Without realising it, my riding skills improved. I was slowly becoming a Hun.

When darkness fell, Tatos took the decision to set up camp. He located a stream with adequate grazing for the horses. "We rest and horses recover. If not camp now, we walk tomorrow because horses dead." No one argued.

Our campsite afforded us an unobstructed view of the approach to the valley. We would be forewarned of an enemy following us.

I found Cai tending to Gordas. To my surprise, his fever had broken. "Do you still have meat that you took from raiders?" Cai asked.

In my haste I had forgotten about the thick pieces of beef I had stashed in the bag two days before.

"Help me boil water. We make broth with meat and herbs I collected", Cai added.

Soon a thick broth was simmering in the pot. Cai fed a generous portion to Gordas, followed by one of his potions. Gordas almost immediately fell into a deep sleep while Cai changed the dressing on his wound. Nodding, the Easterner said, "He recover quicker than I think possible. He ride on own tomorrow, but will be weeks before he walk."

We struck camp before sunrise. I lit the fire once again, and we made sure Gordas consumed a few mouthfuls of the rich meat broth before we departed. Soon we were all mounted and ready to set off. Tatos exchanged words with Gordas, who nodded.

As Cai had predicted, Gordas could now ride unassisted.

"I will lead us to safety", Gordas said. He nodded to Cai and me, giving recognition to our efforts. Huns are not the best at giving compliments, I learned later.

I was confident the Xiong-nu had given up the chase and I felt more relaxed. The world was well again.

As I turned in my saddle to make some comment or other to Cai, I saw it. A cloud of dust was visible at the far end of the valley. My heart sank.

I kicked my horse to a gallop, reined in when I drew level with Gordas, and pointed at the dust cloud.

He did not even look over his shoulder, just scowled and said, "They come, I know. Enemy horses fresher, Hun horses better. We see."

He remained calm, even though he must have been in excruciating pain from his leg wound. I gained respect for the Hun.

Gordas suddenly smiled and said, "Worst happen we fight and die."

I nodded and fell back, realising that the Huns did not fear death in battle, they relished it.

We changed horses as often as always, but the enemy still gained on us.

It was the last watch before sunset when it happened. The horses must have been close to exhaustion when Gordas slowed the pace. He made it clear when he explained, "For horses."

The raiders trailed eight hundred paces behind us. Suddenly the sky turned dark, not unlike a cloud passing overhead and obscuring the sun.

But it was a cloudless day.

I heard it then, the unmistakeable sound of the arrow storm. I reined in my horse and studied the two hundred enemy pursuers. With the arrows still in flight, thousands of horsemen appeared on the ridge of the valley and released another volley.

One moment the Xiong-nu warriors were still there, riding hard, and the next moment all but a few disappeared in swirls of dust and falling horses, as if struck by the invisible hand of a god. The remaining few were struck by the second volley, and they, too, perished. None were left standing.

I was completely dumbstruck. The mystery riders slowly walked their horses towards us. Two riders detached from the horde and rode in our direction. I immediately recognised Bradakos, maybe due to the scowl he wore.

Bradakos rode beside Octar. When Gordas noticed his king approach, he dismounted and went down on one knee. The rest of the Huns in our little band did the same, and Cai and I followed suit.

"Where are your men, general?" Octar asked, looking straight at Gordas.

"They are dead, Great One", Gordas replied.

His words were followed by a long, uncomfortable silence.

The king nodded. "Why are you alive when all but four of my warriors are dead? Explain yourself."

The king listened while Gordas retold the happenings of the past couple of days, including the surprise attack and the rescue.

Again silence ensued. I believe Octar was considering whether to let Gordas live or not.

"You have served me well in the past, general", Octar said, breaking the long silence. "You will accompany us, and I will provide you with an opportunity to correct your mistake."

Gordas inclined his head in agreement and mounted his horse. Octar rode away with Gordas and the Hun warriors in tow, leaving behind Cai, Bradakos and me.

Bradakos looked at me and said, "The fun will soon begin, try to stay alive."

We did not travel farther that day, but made camp for the evening.

Soon after I had lit the campfire, Bradakos and Cai joined me. We were just about to share what remained of our rations when a Hun warrior appeared with a basket filled with fresh meat and an amphora of wine. "King send", he said. "For rescue general. Xiong-nu not need horse anymore."

That evening we feasted on grilled horsemeat and good wine. Although the king had provided the best cuts, we would probably not have noticed as we were famished.

While we relaxed around the fire, Bradakos brought us up to date. "Two days after you had left with Gordas, the king received a report of the presence of a huge Xiong-nu warband in the borderlands. Initially he thought that the problems were caused by small bands of raiders. He immediately gathered a substantial force and we set off in haste. We crossed paths with the horse keepers yesterday and they told us of the ambush as well as your intent to rescue Gordas and the others. Octar is pleased that most of the horses were saved from capture. You have earned his favour. Do not underestimate the gratitude of the Hun king."

Chapter 21 – Meeting

Two days later, we made camp ten miles from where we had rescued the prisoners.

When we had erected our tent, a Hun warrior arrived.

"King say you come now", he said.

The three of us followed the warrior to the tent of the king. He had a small tent set up for his convenience. It was round, and about four paces in diameter. We were ushered inside, finding Octar seated on furs beside the central hearth. He pointed to an area opposite him and said, "Sit."

"For many years, even in the time of my father and my grandfather, small bands of raiders crossed into our lands from the east", Octar said. "I examined the corpses of the warriors who had pursued you. They are of a different people than any I have seen before. Cai Lun of the East, tell me about these people. This new threat."

Cai inclined his head and told his story.

His people, called the Han, live in lands far to the east. The empire of the Han is vast. The people farm the land and stay in fortresses surrounded by massive stone fortifications. To the north and west of the Han live the Xiong-nu, who the Han refer to as the Hu people. The Xiong-nu, or Hu, are much alike Huns. They roam the Sea of Grass with herds of cattle or sheep, and they never stay in one place for long.

The Han and the Hu people have been at war for hundreds of years. Through the ages the Han sent enormous armies to fight the Hu, only for them to be destroyed by the horse archers of the steppes. The Han paid them tribute not to raid their lands, and formed alliances based on marriage. Alas, the raids and retribution continued. The Han are a clever and resourceful people and learned from their mistakes. They developed weapons and strategy and defeated the Hu. They were still a formidable force, but the Han subjugated them.

At the time of Cai's birth, another Hu people, the Xianbei, defeated the Xiong-nu. The remnants of the Xiong-nu began to slowly migrate west. They are a defeated people, but still numerous and dangerous, like a wounded bear. They invaded the land of the Huns to find a place safe from the Xianbei, only to be confronted by the power of the Huns.

When Cai had finished he inclined his head once again.

Octar seemed to be deep in thought, but nodded to show that he was listening. "When we ride to the Xiong-nu today", he said, "you will ride at my side, Cai of the Han. Gather your horses and be ready."

It was mid-morning when the army of the Huns approached the encampment of the enemy. The three of us rode beside

Octar, in the vanguard. As we crested the hill, we saw that the Xiong-nu warriors were mounted - ready and waiting.

The horde of the Huns numbered ten thousand at the least, but did not dwarf the slightly smaller army of the Xiong-nu. The Hun king lifted his hand to call a halt when the forces were five hundred paces apart.

Octar walked his horse down the gentle slope of the hill and motioned for the three of us to join him. His bodyguard of six brutish warriors followed close behind.

He reined in halfway to the Xiong-nu battle line. We did not have to wait long. A small party of equal size detached from their line and started walking their horses in our direction, coming to a halt five paces in front of us.

The Xiong-nu were armed much in the same way as the Huns. I did notice that their bows seemed smaller, though, and their body armour less.

Octar looked at Cai and said, "Give them the words of the king."

"I am Octar, high king of the Huns. You are encamped in the land of the Huns, and have attacked the tribes under my protection."

Cai relayed the words in a tongue that sounded foreign, as if he spoke from the stomach, through the nose.

The apparent leader of the invaders replied via Cai, "I am Panu, the Chanyu of the Xiong-nu, the Son of Heaven. The Xiong-nu are a free people and know no borders. This land belongs only to Tengri, who allows the strongest to survive."

Octar's face showed no emotion. "Panu of the Xiong-nu, the Huns relish battle. My warriors are waiting to be unleashed. They are eager to decorate their saddles with the scalps of the invaders, or honour Tabiti by winning a glorious death in battle."

Panu appeared equally emotionless and replied, "Tengri sends us to this world only so we may die gloriously in battle."

Octar, still expressionless, replied, "Panu, let us visit the smoke tent and allow our spirits to be cleansed. When we are closer to the gods they can show us the way. Like you, I will gladly die in battle today, but let us seek their counsel and submit to their will. Live or die."

Panu remained quiet, obviously thinking on Octar's words. At last he nodded slowly.

Octar growled commands to one of his bodyguards, and the man sped away on his horse.

Both parties waited patiently until the tent was set up. One of Octar's guards arrived with a small, ornate golden bowl filled with seeds. He presented it to Octar who nodded his approval.

The man placed the bowl into a slightly larger one containing glowing coals. He ducked through the opening, appearing empty-handed a couple of heartbeats later.

Octar dismounted and gestured for Panu to follow him. He looked at Cai, and Panu nodded in approval before the three men entered the small tent.

Both the Hun and Xiong-nu parties dismounted and seated themselves on the grass, albeit about fifty paces apart.

The kings seemed to remain in the tent forever. A full watch had passed when Octar shouted for his bodyguard to attend him. The man hurried away and arrived with an amphora of wine, as well as a golden bowl, which he placed on the ground in front of the tent.

Again, we waited for half a watch. Then Octar, Panu and Cai exited the tent.

Octar turned to face the Hun contingent and said, "Panu and I will take the blood oath." Similarly, the Xiong-nu king addressed his people.

The two kings seated themselves cross-legged on rich furs in full view of their armies. Octar filled the golden bowl with wine from an amphora. Both Octar and Panu cut the palms of their right hands with their daggers, closed their fists, and in turn allowed their sacred blood to drip into the wine. They then placed their daggers in the mixture. From each contingent, a champion brought an arrow, plunged it into the wine, and retreated to the ranks.

Octar lifted the bowl to his lips and drank deeply before wiping the red droplets from his scarred face with the back of his hand. The Hun king inclined his head to the gods, and passed the bowl to Panu who mirrored his actions.

"The Huns and the Xiong-nu have an alliance, sealed in the blood of kings", Octar announced. "They will never raise weapons against one another again. The Xiong-nu will settle in these lands and become one with the people of the Huns. They will protect our eastern border and we will come to their aid against any foe too powerful for them to vanquish on their own. For every Hun killed by the Xiong-nu, they will send a warrior to take his place. The Huns gift them the spare horses of the dead warriors. They will live among the Huns."

When his words had been heard by the Huns, he added, "Tonight we will feast."

Panu turned to his people and repeated Octar's words in the Xiong-nu tongue.

The delegations returned to their armies, and great cheers erupted from both sides.

I gained respect for Octar. He was not only a great warrior, but he had the vision to realise that fighting the Xiong-nu would only weaken both sides. Now the Huns's eastern borders were secure and they would turn their gaze to the West. In time.

I was part of the delegation of the Huns that feasted with the Xiong-nu that evening. I drank wine in moderation and ate lots of juicy horse meat. But more than that, I watched and I learned.

Chapter 22 – Life goes on

We returned to the main camp, riding at a leisurely pace, travelling only seventy miles a day. Seventy miles a day would soon kill a Roman horse, and probably the rider as well.

Gordas had regained the favour of the king and was given command of the Xiong-nu warriors who had accompanied the Huns back to their home. The Hun general would integrate them into his own warband.

The people of the tribe had heard about our rescue of Gordas and I was now treated with respect. Like a fellow warrior. When I rode with the Huns, I could hold my own, and there were no more stares of contempt.

Gordas visited one evening. "If I died at hand of Xiong-nu shaman, my shade roam Sea of Grass for eternity. I now have chance to die with blade in hand and go to feast with war god. I teach you Hun way of fighting." He nodded. I nodded, like a Hun. He left.

For a Hun, Gordas really outdid himself. In any event, that is how I became the apprentice to a barbarian general who led a warband which consisted of three hundred Xiong-nu warriors and seven hundred Huns.

The Roxolani are excellent horsemen, some would say as skilful as the Huns. Although they ride equally well, the Huns are tougher men. Their horses and warriors are able to endure extreme hardship. The more time I spent with them, the tougher I became.

Riding for hours until you have no other choice than to sleep in the saddle, yet stay mounted. Where no food is available, blood from your horse, mixed with water, is taken as nourishment. When no water is available, you ignore the thirst. You never give up, no matter what.

Of the battle tactics of the Huns I knew very little.

To the uninformed, it would appear as if there were no tactics, no strategy, but only a milling mass of barbarians who answer to themselves only. That is the genius of the Huns. Deceit.

The cavalry army was divided into groups of ten warriors, called 'arvan'.

The ten men were normally relations from the same tribe, with strong family bonds. Men who had grown up together and lived in close proximity. These 'arvan' were the basic fighting units, with a single warrior in command of each.

Ten 'arvan' together constituted a 'zuun', or a company of one hundred men.

The Huns were not of one tribe, but rather a confederation of tribes. When the need arose, the high king would summon the tribes and they would come together like the fingers on a hand, to form a fist of iron.

The high king required that each chieftain, or tribal leader, train with his men regularly to enable them to be seamlessly levied into the confederate army.

Apart from that, the high king kept a core standing army of two thousand warriors who could be deployed at short notice to counter any unexpected threat.

At this point I must clarify. The Huns were not farmers or civilians who laid down their tools to take up the sword from time to time. Huns were born to make war. They fought bandits who desired to raid their livestock, they fought other wild tribes who shared their territory, and even fought other tribes within the Hun confederation. Huns were in a permanent state of war. War was life. The only variables were the size and the place of the battles.

The commander of the Hun army communicated with his troops by means of a ram's horn. In the dust and confusion on the battlefield, audible signals were the only viable solution.

I spent much time at Gordas's side as he repeatedly practised manoeuvres with his troops, but I also belonged to an 'arvan', and trained as a warrior. We practised to ride as a horde, split into our 'arvan', and attack specific areas of weakness of the enemy. When a gap in the line was created by thousands of arrows, warriors would regroup and pour into the opening, hacking, slashing and releasing arrows at point blank range. All done at incredible speed. The 'arvan' made feint attacks, feint retreats, only for the next wave to hit somewhere else, like lightning. The drills were perfected, and made to look as if chaos reigned. It was the Huns' most terrible weapon. The illusion that they were stupid barbarians without a central command. They were highly trained, elite troops using the most advanced weapons available, and they possessed superior armour in most cases.

Gordas always explained his tactics to me. When to only weaken the enemy with arrows, when to tire them, when to taunt them with a feigned retreat and when to strike like lighting with the iron fist.

I trained with Cai every day. At first the exercises were limited to breathing, and to the training of the eyes. Although I itched for Cai to show me how to handle the sword, he refused. "Warrior who not calm and cannot see blade, is useless. Lucius of the Da Qin, we will train with sword when eyes and breathing good enough. Also learn patience. Patience more dangerous than sharp blade."

I knew that he would never budge, so I trained to breathe and practised my eyesight.

"Stand in front of me Lucius of the Da Qin. Look at my left eye, then hilt of my sword, then my right eye, then my left foot. Do hundred times."

I trained how to move fast and efficient, without boots, of course. Cai made me practise footwork, moving on the outer edges of my feet. Initially I struggled to move smoothly, but after the pain in my soles lessened, I improved. I had to move backwards and diagonally, many hundreds of times a day. All under Cai's watchful eye.

I recall arriving back at my tent one afternoon. As usual, Cai was waiting for me. This time he had two wooden swords tucked under his arm.

"You make good progress, Lucius of the Da Qin", he said. "Today we start with sword."

I was already a master of the sword. I had trained with Nik for at least ten years and with Bradakos for five. Cai handed me a wooden sword and I grabbed it, but he caught me by the wrist. "Grip on sword wrong. Put thumb between third and fourth finger. Only hold with three fingers. Little finger and forefinger loose. Only way to use sword properly, takes time."

Someone who had not seen Cai fight with the sword would probably had burst out laughing, as only a fool would hold a sword with a seemingly weak grip.

I dropped my sword four times that afternoon.

"Remember breathe, remember patience. When hand strong, best grip for sword", Cai explained.

He was right. A month later I felt more comfortable with the grip and I could perform cuts, thrusts and parries, as directed by Cai, without ever dropping the sword.

One afternoon Cai brought a stool and two square cut stones. "I show you", he said, and placed the stones on the stool, about a finger's breadth apart. He took his wooden sword, held it in a rest position, and breathed deeply for a span of heartbeats, calming himself. When he opened his eyes, he stepped forward at speed and thrust the wooden blade between the stones without the blade touching. He continued to execute a series of strikes, all perfectly placed in the gap between the stones.

"Now you do same", Cai said, and stepped back. I just looked at him dumfounded, knowing that to do this was akin to carrying a horse on your back. He smiled slyly, moved forward, and placed the stones about half a foot apart. "Only jest, you start with large gap. Once you do this good, I teach you fight."

I slowly gained control over the movement of the blade. I was no novice after all, but the skill that Cai demanded was of a higher level than my training with Nik and Bradakos. The Easterner's way was almost spiritual, rather than physical only.

Most days I trained with the Huns, and six days a week with Cai. I was young, eager to learn, ate well and slept well. I grew stronger and more muscular, but remained lean. Not unlike the Roxolani warriors. I was half Roxolani anyway.

I did not see Nik and Bradakos every day, but I made a point to visit them once a week. Usually we shared a meal and wine, and discussed my martial training. Cai joined us frequently. Bradakos was interested in the methods that Cai used, although it was clear that he was not convinced.

When I mentioned things like "using grace rather than power" or "letting blows slide off the sword rather than parrying strength with strength" he wore his usual scowl.

"Cai, when you are done with Eochar, you two could come dance for us at a feast night", he said. I knew better and ignored his jests.

Nik and I still spoke Latin when we were alone together. He said that I required no further academic tuition, but when time allowed it, he relayed stories of ancient Roman battles. Afterwards we would share a cup of wine and discuss what could have been done differently.

I began sparring with Cai as soon as I had gained adequate control of the blade. Every time I became carried away with excitement he stopped, and forced me to calm myself through breathing. Soon I could trade blows with him for long periods, remaining calm and relatively relaxed.

I was used to attacking my opponent, then withdrawing, and continuing the fight in this manner. Cai taught me otherwise. "Body move like snake in water. Never stop. Else you will sink. Once engage, do not retreat. To retreat out of fear make unnecessary work for feet. Do not fear, control fight. Stay close and strike with speed of serpent."

My focus improved, my skills improved and most of all, my confidence soared.

But Cai kept me in check. "It good thing to have confidence, but show off not allowed by Dao. Only fight when unavoidable."

Chapter 23 – Time to leave

My year with the Huns was drawing to a close. I had come a long way. I was becoming a man.

The Huns are a resilient people. They are able to endure and survive where others cannot. They are not compassionate or helpful, but they are honourable. Huns rather speak with the bow or the sword than with the tongue. They do not appreciate tall stories or empty lies. Speak only when you have to. Strike out first, then talk.

Some of this rubbed off on me. As a man, I had little time for hollow words. I found it difficult to pity people when I had endured far worse, with very little pity extended to me in turn.

Gordas approached me one afternoon while we were seeing to our horses. "The king wants to see you tonight", he said. "Your man from the East as well. Be at his tent just after sunset."

I bathed that afternoon after I was done with my daily toil, and dressed in a simple tunic. Cai and I made sure we reported to the king's tent at the appointed time. Nik and Bradakos were also waiting, as well as Gordas. The king's guards ushered us inside and showed us to our places. While we waited for the king to arrive, we enjoyed mead. I drank sparingly. No need to explain why, given my previous experience.

The king entered a short while later. We stood and bowed, waiting for him to take his seat. Once he was seated, he gestured for us to return to our seats on the woollen carpets and furs.

"Eochar, you have come to the end of your time with the Huns", Octar said. "You will always be welcome to fight by our side. You have honour and skill. You are a Hun."

This was an exceptionally long speech for a Hun. Even for the king of the Huns.

The king gestured for me to reply.

"The Huns are a people made of iron. I am honoured by your words", I said.

I bowed, the king nodded, and I retook my seat.

Well, with the long-winded speeches done, servants brought plates with enormous haunches of beef which had been grilled over the fire. Amphorae of dark red wine were brought, as well as golden drinking cups. We feasted. Bradakos and Cai spoke mostly with Octar, while Nik and I conversed with Gordas.

Once we had our fill of the beef, the king said, "We have had peace on our eastern border for nearly a year. The Xiong-nu have been true to their word. They have protected our border.

Their enemies have left them alone because they fear the wrath of the Hun."

Octar appeared troubled. "I have many warriors who crave war and combat, therefore I have decided to send Gordas with you when you return to the Roxolani. He will take a thousand warriors with him to assist my brother Bradakos against any invasion from the tribes that test your borders."

Bradakos and I inclined our heads in respect and he said, "We accept with gratitude."

"I will send for their return should I need them", Octar replied.

Again, Octar gestured to a servant. He reverently carried a beautifully crafted horn bow. The servant presented the weapon to me. In the land of the Hun, more value is placed on silver than on gold. The bow was decorated with thin silver wire that also served to strengthen the construction.

"A Hun needs a proper bow", the king said.

I nodded and inclined my head in agreement.

"I have selected twenty good horses from my own herd for you to ride", the king said. "They will remain with you in the land of the Roxolani."

We all inclined our heads.

We feasted till late that night. I had learned to control my intake of mead and enjoyed the remainder of the evening.

The following morning I spoke to Bradakos about the king's wish to send a thousand warriors on loan to the Roxolani. Looking sternly at me he said, "Octar is a man of honour. He is doing this to protect us on our journey home and to keep the band of warriors occupied. Although we did not ask for assistance, we cannot refuse. I trust that Apsikal will not be angered by the sudden arrival of a thousand Huns. We have no choice but to accept. No more talk is necessary."

I felt sad about leaving the Huns. I had become a man during my stay with them. I would miss the tough barbarians of the east.

We departed two days later.

Chapter 24 – Going home

I rode home in the company of Nik, Bradakos and Gordas.

The Huns were now under the command of Bradakos. To sustain us on the journey, we drove a herd of cattle. We had little option but to move at the pace of these beasts, which meant that we only managed twenty-five miles a day. Scouts were regularly sent out to ensure that there were no surprises.

We camped among the Huns, who always set sentries. Not that anyone would like to surprise a thousand Hun warriors.

We encountered few people. As soon as anyone saw us, they disappeared with haste.

Gordas promised death to any of his warriors who antagonised the locals along the areas we traversed. After summarily executing two warriors who had hearing trouble, no further incidents were reported.

Given our slow pace, we made camp early every day. The Huns hunted antelope and wild fowl en route during the day in order to stretch our supply of beef.

Cai and I still trained every day, in private.

One afternoon we ventured from camp, dismounted, and sat down on the grass beside a stream. As was our habit, we sat cross-legged and began our session with breathing and meditation.

After a while, Cai broke the silence. "Today we talk", he said. "We train sword tomorrow."

"I only allowed to pass on martial knowledge to man of Serica, such as myself. This is old rule of my religion since beginning. It to stop enemies of my people to gather knowledge to defeat us. It common sense. Before I left monastery, master call me to attend him. He master of Dao who achieved higher plane of existence, a spiritual man. He told me that I would roam world until my life saved by man who carries bow. He instructed me to pass knowledge of the Dao to this man, although he not of Serica. He also gave me something to keep safe until right moment."

Cai stood, walked to his horse, and retrieved a sword in a scabbard. He handed the weapon to me.

"This a jian, but not ordinary weapon. This sword forged by master swordsmith of Han. Backbone of sword made from extremely hard steel. Two rods flexible soft steel joined on either side. Before they joined, they folded hundreds of times to remove impurities. Once joined, outer edges of steel hardened with fire and ice to make cutting edge that will not blunt. It take years to do. When finished, sword is polished by hand until hot to touch. This happens every day for thousand days. When this done, blade is sealed and no longer requires upkeep."

He pulled the blade from the scabbard. The silvery blade had a blueish glow to it, the tempering line of the edge appearing and disappearing.

"This blade is gift to you from master. He also told me to give you message. That message is not for now. When time is right I will share it with you."

He held the blade in both hands, offering it to me. I reverently accepted it. It felt extremely light. I could barely believe it.

"Speak to no one of this", Cai said. "Use blade only for good."

I nodded. I have known Cai long enough to realise that no words were required.

Days passed without incident.

One evening we sat in front of our tent, as was our habit. I had just lit a fire and Bradakos poured us some wine that he had stashed away.

Bradakos was extremely curious about Cai's fighting abilities and skills with the sword. Until then he had kept his curiosity in check, but he was unable to contain it any longer. "So, Cai, when will you give me a demonstration of your sword fighting techniques?"

"I sorry, Bradakos, my friend. I made oath to Master, only ever to impart knowledge to man chosen by gods. That man Eochar."

Bradakos kept quiet for a while and said, "Do you have any objection to me sparring with Eochar?"

"Eochar has given oath never to train anyone in skills of Dao", Cai replied.

I noticed Bradakos's face fall.

"But I see no reason for you not spar with him, as long as use wooden swords. I not want my friend Bradakos injured." Cai smiled and winked at me. "Show your big brother how it is done."

Nik sipped wine from his cup, regarding the unfolding spectacle with interest.

I had not trained with Bradakos for more than a year. I was keen to evaluate my Dao skills compared to the more traditional ways.

I stood relaxed, in a guard position, my sword raised almost straight above my head with the tip pointing in the direction of my navel. All my weight on my right leg, my left foot raised high.

I had Bradakos confused. "Eochar, I don't want to hurt you."

Cai looked at Bradakos and said, "Pay no attention to Eochar's dancing. Just fight when and how wish."

Bradakos stepped in, drawing back his sword. Cai had taught me how to anticipate the actions of my opponent based on the movement of their eyes and feet. I read Bradakos like a scroll and knew what he was going to do even before he initiated a move. I did not parry the head-high thrust, but used it to my advantage. My new grip allowed me to use the sword as a precision instrument. I met his thrust mid-air with the side of my sword and moved forward, and a little to the right. Just enough for his blade to miss my head and slide along the wooden edge of my training sword.

I angled his blade downward to open him up for my counter, but Bradakos was no fool and he stepped back to regroup. He expected me to step back as well, as would be the norm. But I stepped in and counter cut at his head, not a strike intended to breach his defences. He parried and again I unbalanced him by not allowing the blades to meet edge to edge, his blade just sliding off mine. He stepped back and I moved in, thrusting for his legs. I moved closer as he parried, my blade giving way to his powerful parry, retaining his sideways momentum. I stepped to the right, the power of his parry moving him forward and slightly to my left.

My wrist movements, combined with my new grip, made me lightning fast.

He was still recovering from the parry of my low thrust when my sword moved like a snake, the blade coming to a rest against Bradakos's neck where the jugular enters the skull.

He stared at me in utter disbelief, then nodded, indicating that our bout was over.

Bradakos sat down next to the fire again and I joined him. He filled his cup to the brim and drank deeply, obviously in thought.

Silence descended on the group for at least a hundred heartbeats.

"Eochar, I have never seen anything like that. I have fought and killed countless men. Dangerous men, many the champions of their tribe. From the first ringing of the blades I had always felt the confidence, the knowledge that I would beat them."

He again paused to wet his throat.

"I had never before experienced what I did today. From the first moment that our blades met, I knew you were toying with me. I tried to regroup and disengage, but you kept coming at me, relentlessly."

"I know I am still stronger than you, but it mattered not. You knew which way I would move before I started to move."

The great champion of the Roxolani shook his head slowly.

"Eochar, I am fortunate that you are not my enemy. You are surely touched by Arash. Only the god of war and fire can make a sword move like I have experienced today."

Chapter 25 – Arrival of the man

It took us another moon to reach the lands of the Roxolani.

Bradakos called a halt just inside the borders of our tribal lands. "I will go speak with the king. We have been absent for a year, and now we return with a thousand Huns. To enter Roxolani lands with foreign warriors, I require permission from the king."

Gordas decided to accompany Bradakos.

During their absence, I would command the Huns. It was quite a daunting prospect for an eighteen-year-old, although I had more or less earned their respect. I hoped. They were all aware of my daring rescue of their general, and they also knew that I was a noble of the Roxolani.

But the Huns are brutal. Like the Roxolani, they have nobility, but even noble warriors have to show strength to gain respect.

Bradakos would be away for a quarter of a moon. On the evening of the fifth day I started to relax for the first time. All was well. During the day, I patrolled with the Huns. I did it mostly to keep them busy, rather for fear of some threat or other. In addition we practised cavalry drills. Not much different from my time with the Huns under Gordas.

One of the nobles, a commander of a hundred, was a huge brute of a man called Rhaton. He was an extremely competent warrior, though crueller than most. He wore a cloak fashioned from the scalps of vanquished enemies. It must have taken at least fifty scalps to make a garment of that size.

On the morning of the sixth day, I met with my ten 'commanders of a hundred' to discuss the day's drills.

Like most armies on earth, the Hun army is not based on the outdated Greek system of democracy. In the Hun army, the noble commander tells his sub-commanders what to do. A lenient commander would allow his subordinates to respectfully give their opinions, should he require it.

Rhaton's hundred was sent out to patrol west of our encampment that day. He had a scowl on his face when I gave my commands, but I thought nothing of it. Huns tend to lack humour.

I sent five 'zuun' on patrol, and practised drills with the remainder of the army in the vicinity of the camp. The Huns knew their business, and it was exhilarating to command them. These warriors were without equal.

The sun had not even reached its zenith when I noticed a dust cloud on the horizon. I was unconcerned, as a contingent of Huns was tasked to guard the camp. An enemy would have to get past our patrols as well as the guards. I made a mental note to investigate later in the day.

Our drills did not progress as smoothly the rest of the afternoon. I wanted the manoeuvres to be flawless. We eventually succeeded and headed back to camp, exhausted but content.

It was late in the afternoon. I was dead tired, and permeated with dust. After dismounting at the tent and taking care of my horse, I went to wash in the river. I bathed, allowing the cold water to invigorate my tired body.

I donned a clean tunic that I had brought with me, and walked back to the tent, which was only about fifty paces from the river. Nik attempted to light a fire while it was still light, while Cai meditated a few paces distant. I strapped on my sword belt and walked over to where the rest of the men were encamped.

I was surprised to find Rhaton's regiment already in camp.

A Hun patrol traditionally lasts from first light until last light. The 'zuun' divides into groups of ten, or 'arvan'. These groups of ten are then directed by the group leader. This way they are able to scout a much larger area. They meet again at a pre-arranged location, report back to the leader, and then ride back to camp in one group. Tried and tested.

I waved one of the camp sentries over and questioned him with regards to the arrival of Rhaton's 'zuun'.

Apparently Rhaton and his men had arrived at noon with a dozen slaughtered sheep. They were spitting the sheep above fires. The meat must have been nearly done.

I felt a sudden overwhelming rage rise in me. Barely able to restrain my outward anger, I walked to the tent of Rhaton.

Rhaton stood from his seat near the fire as I approached. "How may I assist the general?" he asked with a mocking smile on his face.

I find it difficult to speak when the demon of anger is rising within me, but I steadied myself and replied, "Explain yourself, Rhaton."

"Explain what?" he said, and stared at me in defiance.

I remained silent. He must have realised that he had crossed a line, and tried to salvage the situation.

"We were riding out to patrol when we came across a flock of sheep. We slaughtered them and brought them back for the benefit of all", he explained.

My eyes drifted to the freshly taken scalp still covered with bloodied blonde hair. Hair like that of my people. Roxolani hair. This was serious. He had attacked the locals and was endangering the diplomatic relationship between the Huns and the Roxolani.

"Hand over the men who took the lives of the Roxolani", I demanded.

At this stage, the men in his 'zuun' had formed a circle around us, watching intently. This must have emboldened Rhaton, and his blood was up.

"Maybe I am the one who did the slaughtering of your people", he said, and his hand moved to the hilt of his sword.

Only a fool would not realise where this was headed, and I had begun to breathe deeply to calm myself. Cai's words came to mind, "Man who fights angry has lost before fight start." I did not reply, but kept on breathing deeply, already feeling the calming effect.

"What's the matter, boy?" Rhaton growled. "Are you too scared to use your tongue? Maybe you should run back to your slanted-eyed priest, or the old man who is your mother."

Cai and Nik had explained it to me in detail. How an enemy would try his utmost to anger me prior to a physical confrontation. Even for one forewarned, it was difficult to control my anger, breathing and all.

But I managed, and a strange calm descended over me. I felt in control of my emotions, and in control of the situation. I decided that I would not take Rhaton's bait. I would not strike at him in anger, but wait for Gordas to mete out punishment on his return.

I looked calmly upon the ranting Hun and said, "Rhaton, you have transgressed. You have ignored the commands of your general and your king. You are nothing, and will face the punishment that you are due when Gordas returns."

He glared at me, his hand still on the hilt of his sword.

I turned around, completely in control of my emotions. As I turned, I heard him draw his blade. I instinctively rolled forward and his sword thrust, aimed at my back, met with air. I drew my jian as I regained my footing. Rhaton had taken a step back, surprised at my agility. The sword felt good in my hand. For the first time I felt what Cai had tried to explain to me, "There is no sword, the sword is everywhere."

I decided not to draw out the fight. Resting in a comfortable guard, I waited for Rhaton to make the first move. I wore no armour. His full armour must have given him confidence.

He stepped in and attacked with a horizontal cut – a predictable move. I retreated a step, barely avoiding his sword which passed an inch from my chest. Rhaton had thought me an easy kill and his careless strike caused him to overbalance, his hand moving past his body. It was the mistake of a novice. My blade came around like lightning and sliced through flesh and bone, severing his hand at the wrist. It was a controlled strike, and as he pulled back in shock, I stepped in and thrust my blade into his neck, just deep enough to sever the spine.

The Roxolani, like the other Scythian tribes, took the scalps and heads of their enemies as trophies. I had never participated in the practice, probably due to my Roman upbringing. I realised in that moment that more than a hundred savage Huns were staring at me and weighing my every move.

I sheathed my sword, picked up Rhaton's sword, and discarded the severed hand. I removed his head in one strike. Using my dagger, I cut slits into his scalp, just above the ears, and proceeded to shake out the skull. I nearly vomited inside my mouth, but on the outside, I was as stone.

I took the bloody scalp by the braid and said to his men, "Take his body and his head to the hill as a sacrifice to Tengri. He was a good warrior. I will not take his skull as a drinking cup."

I looked at the faces around the circle. Without warning the Huns broke out in howls and cheers of approval. That night I had become a man in the eyes of the Huns. Never would any of Gordas's Huns challenge my authority again.

I walked back to my tent on trembling legs and collapsed beside the fire. I realised I still held the scalp of Rhaton by the braid. Nik looked at me in surprise, pointed at the scalp and said, "I see you brought a friend. Who is he?"

"Rhaton, one of my regiment commanders", I said, and accepted the proffered cup of wine.

Chapter 26 – Back with the Roxolani

Bradakos and Gordas arrived back at dusk the following day.

The Roxolani champion came to sit with us at the fire, and Gordas joined his Huns. Bradakos disappeared into the tent to remove his armour and appeared a short while later.

Nik filled a cup with wine and handed it to him. "How is my friend Apsikal?"

"The king is in excellent health", Bradakos said. "He is extremely proud that his nephew has been accepted by the Urugundi. He is more than a little surprised that he is now the host to a warband of a thousand Huns."

Nik nodded and asked, "Are we allowed to join him at the main camp?"

Before Bradakos could answer, Gordas arrived.

"You are welcome, Gordas," Nik said.

Cai stood and poured a cup of wine for our guest. The Hun accepted it with a nod of thanks and sat down beside us.

"Eochar, my men told me what had happened during my absence", Gordas said.

I allowed the Hun inside to surface, and just nodded, staring into the fire. It was clear that Gordas's words made Bradakos curious, but it would have been rude to ask the Hun to elaborate.

For a while we sat in silence. I enjoyed toying with Bradakos.

Eventually Bradakos could not bear it any longer. "So, Eochar the Silent, are you going to share the tale with me?" he asked.

"General, may I ask you to share the tale as told by your men?" I asked Gordas.

My relationship with Gordas was good, as he felt that he owed me a life, so he took no offense and continued. "One of my sub-commanders of a 'zuun' is, or rather, was, a man by the name of Rhaton. A big, cruel brute like me", he grinned. He wasn't jesting, only stating facts.

"Rhaton has always had a problem with authority, but because I had been his commander since he was a young warrior, he always kept his anger in check. Should he have challenged me, I would have killed him on the spot."

He held out his cup and I refilled it from the larger jug. A man telling a tale has a right to wet his throat.

Gordas took a deep swallow and continued. "Rhaton defied Eochar, ignored his commands, and mocked him in front of the men."

Bradakos's face turned red with rage. His anger was never buried deep. It lay just under the skin. Just.

"Eochar did something that no Hun would have done", Gordas said. "He managed to control his temper and decided only to point out to Rhaton the error of his ways."

From the corner of my eye I saw Cai nodding slowly in approval, the corners of his mouth turned down, like a proud father hearing of the accomplishments of his son.

In contrast to that, I noticed a scowl appear on Bradakos's face. Not unlike someone who had just stepped in fresh cow dung with his new boots.

Nik had both his eyebrows raised, like an amused Roman patrician in the forum.

Gordas saw Bradakos's reaction and he played along. "So Eochar just turned around and walked away."

Bradakos now wore a resigned expression. As if he had overcome the shock and made peace with my cowardice.

Gordas decided to end Bradakos's suffering. "Rhaton attacked Eochar from behind. The actions of a coward", he said.

"If I had not seen Cai, the Easterner, fight when I was rescued from the Xiong-nu, I would not have believed what happened next. My men tell me that you slew Rhaton like a champion would kill a dog. He died before five heartbeats had passed, and his scalp now adorns your saddle."

Bradakos was now nodding slowly with approval, mirroring Cai's actions of a couple of heartbeats earlier.

"Eochar, your judgement was sound. You removed a problem that I would have had to deal with eventually."

Then something happened that shocked me even more than Rhaton's attack. Bradakos stood and poured me a cup of wine. He thrust it into my hand and said, "Drink."

* * *

The king of the Roxolani allocated the Huns a portion of land to set up their camp, about a watch from the main settlement, when riding at a leisurely pace. As they were a warband at the command of the king, the Roxolani would supply them with cattle and grain.

The first few days back at the camp of the Roxolani passed quickly. It felt as if I had never been absent. I trained with Bradakos again, and Cai continued to teach me the finer aspects of the sword. Bradakos insisted that we focus on our equestrian skills and archery. When I asked why, he replied, "Do you think that if you trained more with the sword you could have killed Rhaton any quicker?"

I didn't complain. I grew stronger and wiser.

I still visited with Gordas once or twice a week, and continued to practise war craft with the Huns.

Chapter 27 – It starts

We had been back at the Roxolani camp for almost two moons when we were summoned to attend the king.

As was the norm, it was the three of us who enjoyed the trust of the king who were invited to the evening meal.

Bradakos had briefed Apsikal about my stay with the Huns. I could see that he was more than pleased with my progress.

Servants poured red wine into large golden cups and brought platters stacked with grilled beef, bread and cheese. The Scythians did not overcomplicate their food like the Romans, but it tasted delicious. Only the best cuts of meat were reserved for the king.

We ate like kings, and the company was excellent.

I noticed a difference in the way Apsikal spoke to me. I had become a man, and he treated me as such. I was no longer the boy who had left to be fostered by Huns a year and a half ago.

When we had finished our meal Apsikal revealed the reason behind the invitation. "Friends, I am glad for your safe return and more than content that my nephew had distinguished himself during his time with the Urugundi."

"Before you left on your journey, I told you that the despicable Goths are encroaching on our borders", the king added. "What I feared has come to pass. I have received word of incursions along our northern borders. It is only small raiding parties at this stage. They sneak across the border, steal our livestock, kill our people, and run back like the filthy cowards they are. Nephew, what do you suggest?"

"Uncle, allow me to accompany Gordas and his warband to exact revenge on the Goths", I said. "I believe that the presence of the Huns will give them a reason to reconsider their actions."

"I agree Eochar, but I insist that you take Bradakos along. For my own good. If you leave him with me in the camp, I could not possibly endure his sour mood and long face if he is not able to slay Goths", Apsikal replied.

We spoke about Bradakos as if he wasn't there. "Wise words, uncle. I can see that you deeply understand your subjects", I confirmed.

Bradakos scowled and Apsikal grinned.

Nik and Cai remained at the camp. Bradakos commanded a contingent of one hundred heavily armoured Roxolani horse warriors. Each had an apprentice to assist with the armour and the horses. Gordas and I decided to take along five hundred of the fiercest Hun warriors.

The Goths knew the Scythians well. They had clashed with them for years. Not so the Huns, or the exotic Xiong-nu. When you become familiar with the Huns, they lose their scariness over time. I even had Hun friends. Nothing can prepare you for the initial contact, though. They resemble demons with their elongated skulls, overly tattooed bodies, and scarred, beardless faces. Not to mention our Xiong-nu allies with their small slanted eyes, unknown in these parts of the world.

The pace we set was reasonable, to allow the heavier horses of the Roxolani to keep up. The large warhorses were bred to carry heavy loads for short periods of time, rather than for endurance. We did not wish to face the foe with spent mounts.

It took us five days to reach the borderlands. Bradakos knew the area well and he soon identified a suitable campsite with plenty of water and grazing.

Gordas and his men were tasked to scout far and wide to ensure the army was not ambushed. Did I mention that the Urugundi were the best of scouts? Their knowledge of the land and their skills at stealth were equal to the Scythians', but one aspect set them apart. They could somehow endure more hardship. Hun warriors slept outside in extreme cold without complaint. They were able to go without food for days, surviving only on the blood harvested from their hardy mounts without the need or want to light a fire. They would ride with terrible wounds, enduring it in silence, and somehow remain alive to tell the tale. They not only looked like demons – they could become demons when they wished to.

I woke up late on the first day in our temporary camp. It was light, but the sun had not risen yet. Bradakos already had a fire going and was roasting meat of unknown origin. The Huns taught me not to query the origin of meat. It makes eating it easier, most of the time.

"Do not worry. I will not tell your Hun friends that you have grown soft", he said pointing at the rising sun.

You never really knew if he was serious or only jesting. Anyway, I was part Hun, so I just nodded with a blank face. He scowled in reply. Nothing new.

I had just finished my meal, which was delicious by the way, when I became aware of a commotion in the camp. A couple of heartbeats later, Gordas arrived on his horse. He dismounted and approached us.

"My scouts have sighted Goths", Gordas said. "It is a large warband, roughly six hundred warriors. Only one hundred are mounted, though." He smiled like a wolf, aware of the devastation the Huns could inflict upon infantry.

Two hundred Huns, as well as the hundred Roxolani, followed us out of the camp. We knew exactly where the enemy was.

The Hun scout who had located the raiders rode next to me, his saddle adorned with fresh scalps. He noticed me stealing a glance at the scalps and the blood smears on the flanks of his horse. He grimaced, "Do not worry overmuch about the scouts of the Goths."

The Roxolani heavy cavalry rode their spare mounts. Their apprentices followed close behind, each leading a warhorse and a packhorse stacked with armour and weapons.

Two miles from the enemy, the scout signalled a halt. Gordas and Bradakos exchanged words and the Huns trotted away.

Bradakos gave the signal and the Roxolani dressed for war. The Roxolani armoured their powerful horses with chain and scale. Even the heads of the horses were encased in bronze or iron. Once they were mounted, they were almost invulnerable, covered in near impenetrable armour from head to toe.

Bradakos signalled to a couple of his younger Roxolani apprentices to join him. He turned to me and said, "Eochar, are you ready for some fun?" He didn't wait for my answer and set off at an easy pace with ten young apprentices in tow.

"We will ride to the Goths and draw in their cavalry", he said when I drew level with him. "Irritate them with your bow, but don't scare them. If I wished to scare them, I would have taken the Huns along. Only kill one or two. You can join your terrible friends later when they deal with the infantry."

We reined in as soon as we came across the Goth warband, feigning shock at the sight of the host. They were travelling slowly, advancing in an unorganized mass, encumbered by their slow-moving infantry and wagons heaped with loot gained in the lands of the Roxolani. The enemy became aware of our presence almost instantaneously. The cavalry detached from their tribal-bound travelling arrangements and wove through the mass of warriors to get to grips with our small group. Not all the cavalry pursued us, only eighty of the hundred took the bait, the chiefs and nobles disdaining the effort of riding down an insignificant group such as ours.

We wheeled our horses around and rode for our lives, careful not to outpace the enemy, while allowing them to slowly gain on us.

The Goths were spread out, the younger warriors with less mail outpacing the heavier, well-armoured riders.

The Roxolani heavy horses patiently waited in ambush. As we galloped downhill through the centre of a broad valley, they emerged from behind a rocky outcrop, riding boot to boot. Every warrior carried a long, thick wooden lance, tipped with armour-piercing iron. The spear was heavy, and had to be wielded using both hands. Their impregnable body armour negated the requirement for shields.

The Goths were focused on the chase and failed to notice the heavy cavalry approaching from the flank. When the enemy riders eventually became aware of the threat, they came to a slow halt, milling about in confusion. Their actions sealed their fate. Some tried to wheel away from their foe, to no avail. The Roxolani heavy cavalry horses tired easily, but they were bred for speed and power over short distances. Even with full armour, they were able to outpace the winded Gothic horses.

I reined in and wheeled around to watch. The men of metal rode knee to knee in a near perfect line, thundering down on the confused Goths.

Some of them were brave enough to stand their ground and hurl their light spears. But the weapons ineffectually bounced off the heavily armoured Scythians. The rest milled around, undecided. Hesitation during battle inevitably ends in disaster. The Roxolani heavy cavalry passed through them like a wall of glistening metal, not losing their stride, and keeping the line intact.

When the dust settled, all that remained were the corpses of men and the whinnying of dying horses. Heavy cavalry, when wielded with skill, is the most horrific of weapons.

Just then the Huns arrived, whooping and howling like crazed beasts, chomping at the bit to engage with the Gothic infantry.

They rode past us and I fell in at the front of the column beside Gordas. Unlike the Roxolani, the light cavalry of the Huns rode their small Hunnic horses, which were endowed with endless endurance. They did not hold back or try to save the horses - it was not necessary.

The Gothic infantry had time to prepare. They were tall, muscular men with large, round shields, armed with spears and swords. Most wore helmets and chain mail.

Whoever led them was no fool. The Goths deployed with their backs to a copse, their flanks protected by rocky outcrops. They commanded a frontage of two hundred paces, and stood three men deep.

But they were not familiar with the Huns, nor had they experienced the power of their weapons.

We rode at them in a seemingly unorganised mass of riders. At half a mile, instructed by the signal from a horn, we split into two groups of equal number. At four hundred paces from the enemy, each group formed a counter-rotating circle of horsemen, each circle rotating towards the outside of the enemy line - a whirlwind of riders creating dust and confusion.

Again, the horn sounded. In response, the riders peeled away from the outside of the circles and rode towards the enemy line at an angle. Every Hun was equipped with a powerful laminated recurve bow, with at least four arrows in the draw hand and sixty in the quiver. All manoeuvres were executed at breakneck speed, their legs guiding the horses.

At a range of one hundred and fifty paces, the Huns released their first arrows while riding parallel to the foe. They did not shoot randomly, but aimed at a frontage of fifty paces in the centre of the enemy line. As they approached the riders of the other circle, they wheeled away from the Goths, rode parallel with their comrades, and re-joined their circle of death.

This strategy allowed the Huns to pour nearly four thousand armour-piercing arrows into the Gothic formation. The one hundred and fifty Goths in the centre of the line had to face twenty-five arrows per man. Most shafts ended up imbedded in shields, but enough found gaps in their armour, or entered the eyeholes of helmets. Some arrows passed straight through shields, others pierced mail.

The result was total carnage. There was no defence for the Goths who did not use bows. The Huns came around for a second time, and contrary to the expectation of the Goths, they did not turn back towards the circle, but engaged in close-quarters combat, pulling down shields with lassos and striking out with their long-handled battle-axes and slashing swords. It was all over within heartbeats. Hundreds of dead or dying Goths littered the area in front of the copse. Within heartbeats the Huns were among them like carrion birds, taking scalps, hacking off heads and looting the dead. Less than a handful of Huns were dead or wounded.

I sat between Gordas and Bradakos, not taking part in the looting. Bradakos looked on grimly, seriousness etched on his face.

"Gordas, my friend, it is truly like the wrath of some dark, terrible god. This is not war, it is slaughter. I do not think the world is ready for this", he said.

Then he turned his horse and rode to join his men.

Chapter 28 – Meeting the Goths

We spent a moon in the same camp. During that time we engaged two more Gothic raiding parties, with a more or less similar outcome to the first encounter. The Huns were truly terrible in battle. No one could stand against the power of their bows and their savage brutality.

No further raiding parties appeared, consequently Bradakos made the decision to return to the camp of the king.

I sat with him around the fire. "Eochar, the Huns have put the fear of the gods into these Goths", he said. "They will raid no more. But they will be back in force. To overwhelm us with numbers. Mark my words."

"So, what do we do?" I asked.

Bradakos stared into the darkness. "We go back to the king and we prepare. They will come. I will arrange for scouts to stay in this area and report to us regularly."

The Huns were in excellent spirits all the way home. They had taken loot, scalps, and the occasional head of a Gothic champion. Life couldn't be better.

I had much to think about. We had easily defeated the small raiding parties, but the main Gothic army would be a tougher nut to crack. Even with the aid of the thousand Huns, we would be vastly outnumbered.

I decided to discuss the issue with Nik. The Huns are the most terrible of fighters, the Roxolani's heavy cavalry are the best in the known world, but when it came to planning and scheming, rather seek advice from a Roman.

Nik had settled in well with the Roxolani. He was friends with the king and with that came the respect of the tribe. He lived in a spacious tent, and the gold he brought with him from the west could buy him all he desired. I had my own tent close to Nik's, but most evenings I found myself joining him in his comfortable surroundings, sharing a meal and good wine.

Nik stared into the fire and took a long swallow from his cup of red wine. "I doubt whether the Roxolani on their own would be able to defeat the great armies of the Goths", he said. "They are just too numerous. We could ask for Roman assistance, but I would not recommend it. Once you have invited the wolf into the fold there is no going back."

"We could ask the Huns to support us against the Goths. The Roxolani might have to join the Hunnic confederation to achieve that. It seems the choice comes down to deciding which is the lesser of two evils, or glorious death in battle as a third alternative. Though, as a Roman, it is not my way."

A Roman would have replied immediately. The Scythian and Hun ways had rubbed off on me, and I just sat there, sipping my wine, thinking through the alternatives.

"Nik, I am part Roman and would prefer Roman rule, but the Roxolani are horse people, not so different from the Huns. They would lose their soul under Roman rule, but prosper with the Huns. But there is another alternative. Peace with the Goths, without bending the knee to them, if that is at all possible."

Nik drank deeply and I could see his thoughts were equally deep. "It is worth a try", he said. "War remains a terrible thing. Terrible, but sometimes necessary. I am sure that the Goths would want to talk before fighting us. We can however not ask for parley, as that will show fear and weakness. Remember, this is not your burden to carry. Apsikal is the king, not you."

* * *

Before three weeks had passed, we were summoned to the tent of the king. Seated opposite me was Nik, Cai and Bradakos, of course.

"To complicate the matter, the Goths have requested to meet with me", Apsikal said. "They are arrogant. The request to meet carried the tone of a summons, or even an order. I cannot accept. It will show weakness, and a desire to make peace. The Goths know that they are more numerous than us, but they know our horse warriors are without match. And they fear our allies, the hordes of the East."

He took a sip from his cup of mead and continued. "To strengthen the border, I have arranged that Irbis, one of the local nobles, assemble the army of the North. They are camped close to the border to ensure that the Goths do not start raiding again after you have dissuaded them."

A silence fell over the meeting. Nik drank deeply from his cup and said, "Apsikal, I am a Roman. Rome conquers not only by strength of arms. They conquer by guile and deceit. Send me to the Goths, together with Bradakos and my son. We will be your ambassadors and you will not have to lose face."

"Your suggestion has merit", the king said, "but I do not like placing your lives in danger. The Goths are an untrustworthy lot. They could kill you on a whim."

"Apsikal, you know that your nephew needs experience if he is to take over from you one day. This is a good opportunity for him to watch and learn", Nik replied.

Bradakos grunted in agreement. "Maybe I can kill a couple of the filthy Goths before the Roman talks them to death." He smiled his awkward smile to show his bad attempt at humour. Or maybe he wasn't jesting. One never knew with Bradakos.

Two days later, Nik, Cai, Bradakos and I departed from the tented village, accompanied by an escort of Huns led by Gordas. We were on our way to the land of the trees, the land of the Thervingi Goths.

The journey north was uneventful and I remember little of it. I spent quality time with my friends. Nik told us stories of the time he and Apsikal spent in Rome as companions of the emperor.

It took ten days to reach the borderlands and a Roxolani tented village next to the Hierasus River. As a Roman, you tend to think that the people we call barbarians are backward and unorganised. Not so. A distant cousin of the king, called Irbis, was the tribal leader of the area bordering the lands of the Carpi. He was an impressive man, and no doubt a capable warrior and commander of men. A messenger from the king had reached him a few days earlier so he knew who we were and why we came. He also knew Bradakos, who later explained to us that he had fought side by side with Irbis on more than one occasion. "He is a good warrior. It is the reason why he commands the northern army. Roxolani men will not follow a weak leader, unlike the Romans", Bradakos said, and fixed Nik with a sidelong glance.

The Roxolani's northern army was at the ready. They were camped less than five miles from the river.

Although we couldn't see the army from our designated place of parley, it boosts your confidence to know that five thousand of the best horse warriors in the world are close by should you be in need of them. Equally, my newfound confidence was dented when we found out that the Goth army was nearby and that they numbered nearly fifteen thousand men.

The Carpi and the Goths had a camp on the opposite side of the river. We sent a messenger to the Goths to let them know that the envoy of the Roxolani had arrived.

That evening we feasted with Irbis and his commanders. It was more of a war council than a feast, so we ate well and drank little. "The Goths do not have an alliance with the Carpi," Irbis explained. "The Carpi has submitted to the Goths, who are migrating their people westwards from the forests to the northeast. They are here to conquer land for their people. They are here to subjugate us - to bring us under their heel. I have sent a message to the king, requesting that he mobilise the rest of our army. The reason they requested a parley was to allow time for their forces to gather. I have informed the king of this as well."

Irbis stared into the fire. "We need the help of the fearsome Huns. The host of the Goths is too numerous. We need to unleash the power of the armies of our Eastern allies on these invaders. The gods help us."

Nik interrupted and said, "Irbis, we will meet with the Goths soon. What do you want us to achieve? Do we stall them or do we lure them to attack before their forces are mobilised?"

"Roman, the only way we can defeat them is to draw them into our territory. We have to engage them and hurt them. Then we feint a retreat. We draw them in, link up with our main army, and annihilate them with the help of our allies." He looked at Gordas and nodded. "We use cavalry only, therefore we are mobile. The Goths rely on infantry."

Irbis grinned evilly and said, "To answer your question, Roman, go meet with the Goths and do what comes naturally to you Romans. Annoy them."

The negotiations were to take place on an island near the centre of the river at a place where the river could be forded. The Goths had set up a tent on the island, in full view of our archers. It was a peace parley so none dared to risk the ire of the king, although I imagine that most of the archers considered releasing a shaft or two.

I don't always understand why the Goths and the Scythians hate each other. Goths are fearsome warriors, like the

Scythians, but I guess that there are two things that set them apart. Firstly, Goths farm the soil. A Scythian only digs in the soil if he is burying treasure, or the dead. Working the soil is degrading to a Scythian and they believe it to be an affront to the gods.

Scythians revere seven gods, but primarily the god of war and fire. Arash is the only god whom temples are built for. The Goths worship Teiwaz, also the god of war in their culture. Often, in life, people who serve totally different gods are more forgiving towards their respective religions than peoples who serve virtually the same god under a different name with slightly different fundamentals. Take the Roman god Mars and the Greek god Ares for instance. Virtually the same, but the Greeks treat Mars with contempt and revulsion, which doesn't really help to unite the cultures, if you know what I mean.

In any event, the Scythians hated the Goths and the Goths found the Scythians repulsive. The backdrop to the get-together wasn't really cause for celebration.

We didn't have to wait long. We could see the Gothic delegation arrive on the other side of the river. A messenger soon requested our presence.

Theoretically, we should not have carried weapons, but Bradakos said, "I will not be in the presence of Gothic filth without a weapon. They are scheming and treacherous. They will have weapons concealed - it is their tent."

Nik tried to reason with Bradakos, but he was not to be persuaded, so a very nervous messenger left to inform his lords that four men, armed with swords, would be attending the parley. Cai remained at the camp, but we took Gordas along, for effect.

Nik went over the plan with us again before we forded the river on our horses to meet with the enemy. My father was dressed in a simple, white cotton tunic and a soft fur cloak. He wore no armour. "My age is my armour", he said, and smiled. "At my age I am always ready to die."

Bradakos was dressed in full armour. Nik at least persuaded him to leave his helmet at our camp site. As I explained before, he was not one for show, but revelled in practicality. He wore a long-sleeved scale armour shirt that extended to his knees. Not the traditional bronze or iron scales of the Romans, but scales made from filed down horse hooves. According to Bradakos it was light, much stronger than metal, and required very little maintenance. He insisted that it turned an arrow much better than metal. He wore greaves of iron. His forearms were protected by vambraces made from boiled leather, reinforced with metal strips. The leather was undyed, of course. To round off the picture, he donned a fur cloak made from the skin of a brown bear.

On the insistence of Bradakos, I was similarly dressed. The horse-hoof scale armour was a present from him. After he assisted me to don my armour and cloak, he looked me over and scowled in a satisfactory manner, if that is at all possible. "Good. Dressed like a man, not a fancy bird", he growled.

Gordas regarded us with interest and removed his tunic, thankfully not his leggings as well. From his saddlebag he took a cloak made from human scalps. I couldn't help but flinch. His body was scarred with many cuts, similar to those on his beardless face. The areas not disfigured with scars were excessively tattooed. He noticed my inquisitive stare.

"When our friends die in battle, we mourn them with the blood of warriors, not the tears of women", he explained.

I flinched again.

The Goths were waiting for us close to the tent. They were still mounted. We came to a stop about ten paces from them.

There were four of them, mounted on good horses. Not of the same quality as those of the Roxolani, but then the Roxolani had the best horses in the known world. Most Huns would disagree.

All four warriors wore mail armour. Short-sleeved, but extending to the knees, with slits on the side to facilitate riding. One of them wore a lamellar shirt with bronze scales in addition to his mail. All sported splinted greaves and vambraces.

They were big men, larger than us, with blonde hair and thick brown beards. Mayhap not taller, but broader and more muscular. It seemed that they were bigger boned than us, with bigger hands, thicker wrists and ankles. Although they were covered in armour, I could see their thick necks and the muscles on their forearms rippling as they handled the reins. They were nobles and warriors all. The warrior with scale armour was older, maybe forty summers, while the other three were younger by ten.

I immediately noticed the effect Gordas had on the Goths. While their eyes passed over us, it lingered on Gordas, but, to their credit, they did well not to show the fear which they obviously felt. If you see a Hun for the first time and you are without fear, you are probably dead already.

As if rehearsed, all of us dismounted at the same time. The lead Goth with the scale armour gestured for us to follow him into the tent. He was clearly in charge of the delegation.

The tent was an opulent affair. The ceiling was high, with a smoke hole in the middle. A multitude of soft furs served as carpets. Two low tables were placed opposite each other on either side of the fire burning in the central hearth.

The Goths walked and seated themselves behind one of the low tables, sitting cross-legged on the furs, and gestured for us to do the same. We obliged and sat down opposite them.

The lead Goth gestured to the attending slaves to pour wine.

Allow me to digress. There is little trust to go around at a meeting like this. Poets speak of valour and honour and "rules of parley" governing such a meeting. In reality you are seated opposite people whom you would rather kill than talk to. Which happens often, that is, killing rather than talking. Therefore the need for neutral ground like the middle of a river.

The slave poured the wine from a silver jug, dividing it into eight silver goblets. He showed us the full glass and summarily consumed it. To the surprise of no one. He sat down in the corner to show us that he wasn't dying from some evil poison. The lead Goth drank his wine first, to confirm that there was no foul play. We all followed suit. Everyone knows that it is impossible to parley if you are too sober.

The Goth leader spoke in passable Scythian. "I am Buruista, the reiks, or war leader, of the Goths. I command here and these are my generals", he said, and gestured in the direction of the others seated at the table. "I have met the king of the Roxolani before, but I do not see him among you?"

As discussed prior to the meeting, Bradakos spoke first. "Our king has sent me, Bradakos, his general, to do his bidding. Our king is not a house slave to be ordered around on a whim, Goth. This young man is Eochar, kin of the king, and the old man is Nik, the ambassador of the Romans and a friend of the Roxolani." As rehearsed, he did not mention, neither did he introduce Gordas, which visibly unsettled our hosts.

I could see that Buruista was unsure of how to proceed. It is one thing to fight the Roxolani, it is another to attack allies of Rome. Even though Rome was in turmoil, they still ruled most of the known world.

The reiks recovered quickly, though, and continued. "Our nation is in need of farmland to feed our people. The lands to the north no longer sustain our vast people. We outnumber your armies ten to one and we could easily slaughter them, but we are a fair and peaceful people and therefore we have come to seek a treaty." The Goth drew breath and continued. "We will allow the Roxolani to remain where they are. There is enough grassland to sustain your horses and cattle. Your way of life will be retained. All that is required is that your king kneels before us, and become a vassal of the Goths. Then you will be allowed to live and to prosper."

"So, Scythian, what will it be? Life or death?"

What do you say to that? I was shocked and a bit taken aback, but my face remained expressionless. I watched the Goths closely. Two of the reik's henchmen were clearly generals, and keenly following the conversation. I could see the intelligence in their eyes. But the third man worried me. He had a different look about him. Not intelligence, but violence. I think the gods spoke to me or gave me the wisdom to see it. This man was brought to challenge and kill us. He was no general, he was a fighter, a killer. I could not allow this to happen.

Call it the stupidity of youth, call it my Roxolani heritage or anything you wish, but before my brain could intervene, I said, "It sounds to me like the whining of a coward, this talk of peace." I looked straight at the killer. He kept my gaze without reacting. That is when I realised he didn't speak our language.

But the reiks and his legitimate generals turned red in the face. Nik placed his hand on my leg, as if to restrain me, and Bradakos scowled. No surprise there.

"You have forfeited your life, boy", the reiks growled.

I suddenly felt strangely calm, when heartbeats before I was bristling inside with anger. I looked at the reiks and said, "I will fight any of you. If I win you leave."

Then Bradakos surprised me. He stood, also a huge insult by the way, and pointed at the killer.

"Let the boy fight your champion", he growled. "We will take the blood oath."

Bradakos hesitated for a moment. "Or would you prefer to fight this man", he said, and pointed at Gordas.

The leader of the Goths replied, "The boy insulted us. He will fight."

"So it will be", Bradakos replied.

The leader of the Goths nodded, clearly relieved that his champion did not have to fight Gordas. This was an easy way for them to get what they wanted and not lose warriors in a pitched battle.

I pointed out the differences between the Scythians and the Goths, but there is one ritual they both hold sacred. An oath, especially an oath with blood involved.

Bradakos unsheathed his dagger and pulled it across the inside of his palm. He then balled his fist and held the jug of wine underneath, allowing the blood to drip into the wine. Each man at the meeting repeated the action. Then the slave poured us each a goblet of the wine mixed with blood. He drank deeply, followed by each man in turn.

Bradakos stood and said, "We are now bound by the sacred blood oath. Should your champion defeat the boy in single combat, then we will share our lands with the Goths and bow the knee to them, else you will leave and never set foot in our lands again."

That was the easy part.

We went outside to prepare for the duel.

Bradakos took me aside. "Don't kill him too quickly", he said. "Give us a bit of a show. Gordas will enjoy a good show."

The Goth was slightly shorter than me, but a lot broader. He had no neck to speak of, just an immensely thick, short separation between his torso and his head. He was no petty tribal warrior, but the terrible champion of the Goths. Best of thousands. Many gold and silver rings adorned his arms and fingers. Evidence of his success.

I breathed, and emptied my mind.

He was supremely confident. Wasting his breath by insulting me in his native tongue, rolling his huge shoulders. He wore full armour, and donned his helmet as well. He was taking no chances. The Goth slowly drew his blade, the patterns dancing in the light, the mark of its quality.

Against the advice of Bradakos, I left my helmet with Nik. I slowly drew my jian from its tight-fitting scabbard. A simple blade, but few better had ever been made.

He came at me with lightning speed, revealing his intentions late. I recognised the move, a horizontal cut, from left to right. The power behind it was immense, and even if I parried it, it would most likely have swept my blade aside.

I decided to do the improbable. It would not be a test of swordsmanship, but rather a test of swords. I waited until the last moment and stepped to my left and back, away from the Goth, drawing the blade back above my left shoulder, exposing my abdomen. As his sword cleft the air in front of my chest, I stepped forward and brought down my jian, feeling the power surge through my spine into the sword. The blade struck like a bolt of lightning from the hand of a god, severing the Goth's blade four inches from the hilt. I saw the disbelief in his eyes as I stepped in, my blade entering his open mouth just deep enough for the tip to cut into the spine.

The eyes of the Goth champion glazed over and he fell forward, facedown in the dust.

Total, absolute silence descended over both parties who were watching the duel.

I inclined my head to the Goths and walked over to my friends. Nik looked relieved. Gordas looked at me suspiciously, like he found out a secret that I had kept from him. Bradakos smiled and said, "Good show."

The Goths walked to their horses and rode away without another word.

"Well done, I believe you have just negotiated a peace treaty with the Goths", Nik said dryly.

Later, we abandoned the camp by the river and joined the rest of the army at the main camp.

The news of the defeat of the Gothic champion had spread like wildfire through the camp, and everywhere the warriors were feasting.

Even though the fight had only lasted a couple of heartbeats, I felt exhausted and was in no mood for a celebration. Gordas joined the Huns who escorted us, while Cai, Nik and Bradakos were having their own little private get-together in front of the tent we all shared.

I excused myself and started towards my sleeping furs in the tent. Nik motioned for me to wait and said, "Before you go, let us talk for a short while."

I reluctantly sat down and Nik said, "Bradakos, the Goths took the blood oath. Will they leave?"

"Nik, the blood oath is sacred to the Goths and the Scythians. They will not attack us", Bradakos stated as a fact.

Nik looked at all of us in turn. "I am a Roman and will make and break oaths as it suits me. That is our way."

Cai nodded in agreement. "My people same. Not place my trust in words", he said.

Bradakos waved away our concerns. I nodded and retired to my furs. All around me I could hear laughter as our warriors feasted into the night.

Chapter 29 – Betrayal

I woke with a hand of iron clasped over my mouth. I panicked for a moment, but realised that it was Cai, keeping me from making a sound.

He held his finger to his lips in the universal sign for silence.

He moved to wake Nik, but I stopped him just in time. I kicked Nik's foot and he quietly came upright, the blade of a dagger gleaming in his left hand. Cai nodded his thanks.

He woke Bradakos silently.

Cai motioned for us to ready our weapons.

As soon as we had retrieved our weapons, Bradakos and I slipped on our scale armour. Unlike metal scale armour, the hoof scales make no sound to warn enemies.

Cai whispered, "Enemy warriors in camp, among tents. Ready yourself."

A piercing scream broke the silence. A mailed warrior burst into our tent with a sword in the one hand and a club in the other. His eyes widened as he met with four armed men, fully alert and awake.

It is strange how people have an unspoken understanding. We were all expert swordsmen, but we agreed that Cai was the best. Without a doubt. Bradakos, Nik and I just stood frozen while Cai moved like a viper. In the confined space, the intruder ended up with a sword through his neck, dying instantly. A heartbeat later a second warrior burst into the tent wielding a short battle-axe. Cai performed an almost flawless repeat of the first move. If it weren't a life or death situation it would have been funny. In the dark I noticed a ghost of a smile play around Bradakos's lips.

Outside, all hell broke loose. Goths had killed the half-drunk sentries and infiltrated the camp. Most of the Roxolani warriors were intoxicated from wine or mead consumed at the victory feast. Unawares and unable to respond.

Goths entered tents and unceremoniously slew sleeping Roxolani warriors. Some managed to get their hands on swords, bows or axes and fought back bravely, but the numbers of the Goths were overwhelming. The Roxolani warriors are used to fight from the back of a horse and they have immense skill, but on foot, outnumbered and dull-witted from feasting, they were no match for the infantry of the Goths.

It was a massacre, not a battle.

We exited the tent and were noticed immediately. A group of ten Goths came running at us from the chaos. They died to a man in a few heartbeats. Now Bradakos was smiling. Broadly.

Nik yelled, his voice rising above the noise, "The army is lost, we must try to reach the horses."

Bradakos took the lead and we weaved through the tents to where our horses were kept. Along the way we encountered small groups of the foe and killed them all.

At last we burst out of the chaos of the camp, but the horses were gone, and from the gloom, about forty Goths appeared.

Bradakos looked at us and said, "Die well, my friends, I will see you in the feast-hall of the gods."

The Goths advanced in battle formation. They were taking no chances. Shields overlapping and spears and swords at the ready. Our fate was sealed.

As the leader advanced and raised his spear, he suddenly disappeared under hooves as a howling Hun broke through the line of warriors. Heartbeats later the Goths fell in a storm of arrows. The ones still alive were trampled into the ground by the horses of the howling warriors. Most Huns dismounted, took scalps and looted, ignoring the Goths from the main camp closing in on our position.

Gordas appeared from the dark, leading four Hunnic horses.

We quickly mounted and followed the howling Huns from the camp. I could see hundreds of Gothic cavalry following us into the night. Gordas just glanced over his shoulder, released a couple of arrows blindly, and said, "Let's see if they can ride like Huns." I heard a scream as one of his arrows found flesh.

Needless to say, the Goths soon gave up the chase. "They cannot even catch Roxolani", Gordas said.

Bradakos scowled and asked, "How did you escape the Goths?"

"We camped away from the Roxolani, in the hills. Drunk Roxolani and drunk Huns do not always mix well. My scouts woke us", Gordas informed us bluntly. "Roxolani trust too much", he added for good measure.

"I believe you are right, my friend", Bradakos said. "I should have known this would happen. The Goths have no honour."

Once the euphoria of escaping certain death had faded away and was replaced by fatigue, the grim reality of what had happened dawned on me. The army of the North had been annihilated.

The land now lay open to the marauding host of the Goths. They could pillage, loot and murder at will, with only old warriors and boys to swat aside.

As always, the Huns had spare horses for all, and we made excellent time. I was used to the unforgiving pace set by the Huns. I noticed that Nik was struggling, but the old man had iron in his veins and he did not fall behind. Mind you, even Bradakos struggled a bit, although he would rather have died than admit it, or complain about it.

We called a halt when the sun was low in the sky. There was no way the Goths could reach us. No other breed of horses could have covered the distance, not even close. The little Hun horses were tough as nails, and never tired.

When we found an appropriate spot with water and grazing for the horses, we dismounted and set up camp. Even after such a gruelling day of riding, a few of the Huns galloped off to forage for food. They returned with an antelope, as well as a mixed bag of wild fowl and a couple of hares.

The Huns might be barbarians of the cruellest kind, but they know how to prepare a delicious pottage. They mixed wild roots and herbs with the meat and soon we feasted like kings.

After our small group retired to our own fire, Nik conjured up a skin of wine. I looked at him, the question written on my face.

"You took your armour. I salvaged this", he replied, and took a long swallow.

Chapter 30 – Decision of the king

The Goths had neither the skills, nor the quality of horses to catch up with us.

Due to the urgency of the matter, we wished to immediately report to Apsikal as soon as we arrived at the main camp of the Roxolani. Although dust and sweat permeated every conceivable orifice of our bodies, we headed straight to his tent.

Two mean-looking guards flanked the door of the king's tent. On our arrival, one disappeared inside and emerged a couple of heartbeats later. We were ushered into the presence of the king.

Apsikal looked old. He was pacing up and down, concern etched on his face.

The king needed little intuition to realise that we had ridden for days to bring urgent tidings. Apsikal gestured for us to sit. Servants handed us cups brimming with wine.

We waited for him to speak first.

"I can see that you bring urgent tidings. Speak"

Bradakos went down on one knee and said, "My king, we arrive with dire news." Bradakos was not one for mincing words.

"Eochar had defeated the champion of the Goths in single combat, thereby securing a Goth withdrawal, sealed with the blood oath. While we were celebrating our victory, the Goths broke the sacred oath and overran our camp in the middle of the night." He nodded in the direction of Gordas. "The only reason for our escape is the valiant efforts of Gordas and the Huns. The entire army of the North has been annihilated."

Apsikal was visibly distraught. He poured himself a goblet of red wine from a beaker and downed it in one swallow. The pouring servant looked on, confused and worried.

"The entire army? Five thousand warriors?" he asked.

Bradakos nodded.

Apsikal's shoulders slumped and he sighed deeply.

Bradakos hung his head and said, "My king, it is my fault. Nik warned me that the Goths would break our sacred oath, but I did not heed his words."

The king nodded. "They have broken the blood oath, you are not to blame. We must honour Arash with the blood of those Goths. They must pay for this, one way or another. I will sooner die than allow these oathbreakers to settle in the lands of our forefathers."

"There is only one option that remains", he said. "We must ask Octar of the Urugundi for assistance. Bradakos, you and Eochar will go to Octar. I know you see him as a brother. He will not refuse you. I will stay to lead the remainder of the army. I will gather our people and livestock. We will evade the marauding Goths, and with the help of Gordas and his men, we will hold out until your return. Rest tonight and leave early tomorrow morning."

I went down on my one knee next to Bradakos and said, "We will do as you command, but we would leave now with a small escort of Huns. No time is to be wasted."

Apsikal nodded in agreement. I embraced Nik and Cai, and we rode for the camp of the Huns.

The hardy Hunnic mounts devoured the miles. Our bodies were as hard as rock by then and we rode with grim determination. The outcome of our mission would determine the fate of my people. We encountered few along the road. Once or twice we noticed a group of bandits in the distance who immediately disappeared once they laid eyes on the heavily armed and armoured riders with the elongated heads and scruffy outlandish horses.

We brought many spare horses and managed eighty miles every day, arriving in the land of the Huns before the passing of half a moon. We talked little during the journey, all of us preoccupied with our own thoughts. Bradakos blamed himself for the fiasco, therefore he didn't even scowl at me. I started to pity him, but I knew it was something that I could not help him with. Showing my concern for his emotional state would just make it worse, so I rather kept my mouth shut and left him brooding.

A Hun patrol intercepted us a day's ride from the camp. We were recognised almost immediately. They escorted us to the king at speed.

It would have been folly to demand to see Octar immediately, it is not the way. We could only ask, and hope that the request reached Octar's ears sooner than later.

The gods were with us, though, and only half a watch passed before we were summoned to the king.

Bradakos and I were ushered into the opulent tent of the great man, king of the Urugundi and overlord of the Hun confederation. He immediately waved away his guards and gestured for the servants to pour wine and leave the tent.

We both went down on one knee, but he in turn clasped our forearms in the warrior's way and raised us to our feet.

"We are alone, there is no need for decorum", Octar said impatiently. "Bradakos, my brother, tell me why you have death written on your face."

Bradakos shared the tale with Octar, who grew red in the face when he mentioned the breaking of the blood oath. His hand moved to the hilt of his sword. Although he was a king, he was still a Hun. Quick to anger, slow to forgive.

"The Roxolani are a defeated people, Octar. It is due to the oath-breaking Goths and my misplaced trust", Bradakos said.

Octar frowned, "I can see that your mind is ridden with guilt. Bear it like a warrior, like you would bear the pain of a wound. Accept the will of the gods. Soon we will unleash the wrath of the Hun on these people, these toilers of the earth. We will wash away your guilt with the blood of the Goths."

He held up his hand to show that we should wait, and he left the tent. I could hear him converse outside, and a short while later he returned.

"I have summoned the army of the Urugundi and its allies", Octar said. "The Hun horde will gather. Time will not be wasted. Within seven days we will be ready. Rest now. We will discuss the detail before we leave."

Octar assigned us a comfortable tent to share, and servants took care of our horses.

Bradakos and I went to the river to wash the sweat and dust from our tired limbs. Afterwards we donned clean tunics and handed our dirty clothing and armour to servants for cleaning. Our weapons we would take care of ourselves.

When the sun set, Octar sent us platters of beef and wild fowl. We washed it down with an amphora of purple-coloured red wine from Persia.

The week that followed was one of the longest weeks of my life. While the Huns gathered their army from across the land, all Bradakos and I could do was eat, drink and brood.

On the sixth day we were summoned to the king.

"My army will be fully assembled by tomorrow", Octar said. "We will leave the day after, early in the morning. The army will travel light. Each warrior will have only two spare horses. I will accompany my men and speak with king Apsikal in person."

True to his word, the Hun army departed on time. Twenty-five thousand of the best horse warriors in the world, set on revenge.

It took three gruelling weeks to return home – a large army is inevitably slower than a small group of riders.

The Roxolani were on the move, camping at a different location nearly every day. Apsikal had not been idle. From all corners of the land, different sub-tribes and families had been gathered, as instructed by the king. There is safety in numbers. The gathered people were safer against attacks from the marauding Gothic warbands.

Our scouts located the Roxolani camp with little difficulty. Apsikal and Bradakos had discussed the planned route beforehand and he had a good idea where they would be camped. Finding a suitable campsite for the Hun army proved to be more challenging. As every warrior had three horses, the animals numbered seventy-five thousand. Octar ended up splitting his army into groups of five thousand, forming a protective screen around the Roxolani.

Once the Huns were settled in, Apsikal extended an invitation to Octar to join him. Bradakos and I accompanied Octar and his retinue of bodyguards on their visit to King Apsikal.

To show respect, the king of the Roxolani rode out to meet Octar. Apsikal was immaculately dressed in full armour, resembling a shining god.

The parties rode to within twenty paces of each other. Both Apsikal and Octar dismounted, followed by their respective retinues, walked towards each other, and clasped forearms in the way of the warrior. They mounted again and rode to Apsikal's camp, deep in discussion. We afforded the kings at least thirty paces to allow them to converse in private.

When we arrived at the king's tent, Apsikal and Octar entered. They both gestured to their retinues not to follow.

Servants entered with wine and trays of meat and cheese.

I made myself comfortable outside the tent, expecting the discussions to be lengthy. To my surprise, a servant appeared within a quarter of a watch and respectfully told Bradakos and me that the kings requested our presence.

Servants handed us golden goblets filled with red wine. Octar took a swallow of the wine and said, "Your king and I have reached an agreement. Together we will punish the Goths for their treachery, and chase them from the lands of the Roxolani. In exchange for our help, the Roxolani will join the Hunnic federation. That means that I will be the high king, your overlord."

I wondered where this conversation was heading.

"Octar had agreed not to interfere with the governance of our people, apart from calling on our army to render assistance when required", Apsikal said. "There is, however, one further condition."

Apsikal's eyes struggled to meet mine for a heartbeat, and then he said, "Bradakos will be my successor. He is like a brother to Octar."

Neither Apsikal nor Octar apologized to me. It was not the way of the Scythians. The high king desired Bradakos to be the next king, so his wishes had to be respected.

Bradakos appeared utterly shocked.

When we had exited the tent, I turned to him and said, "Bradakos, you are like an older brother to me. I grew up as a labourer on a farm and never dreamt that I would become a noble of the great nation of the Roxolani. I do not need to become their king. You have my full support. There is none better than you to lead them in future."

That evening I shared the happenings of the day with Nik and Cai.

Cai drank from his beaker and said, "Life not something we able to control. Not let thoughts linger on lost kingship. It not meant to be."

I slept fitfully that night, and went for a ride on my own early the following morning. By the time I arrived back at the camp, I felt relaxed and free from negative thoughts. For the time being, I would focus on the plight of the Roxolani people. Who knew what would follow?

Chapter 31 – Hunting with Bradakos

The Roxolani had evacuated their northern pastures. These lands were now infested with roaming bands of Goths, scouting the way for the main body of warriors.

It was time for action. Apsikal called a council of war and I was invited.

We all gathered in the spacious tent of the king.

Although Octar commanded the majority of the host, it was Apsikal's territory and he spoke first.

"The Roxolani army is ready. In total, we have seven thousand warriors. Two thousand are heavily armoured and the rest is light cavalry", Apsikal said. "The Goths are devious and we will commit a grave mistake should we underestimate them. First, we have to determine the size and location of the Goth army. Secondly, the arrival of the Huns must not be discovered by the Goths."

"Bradakos, I need you to accompany Eochar, and take the best scouts of the Roxolani with you. Bring me the information I require", Apsikal added.

The king deferred to Octar of the Huns who was standing beside him, and nodded.

"The Huns will protect the camp of the Roxolani. Our scouts will find the Gothic scouts and deal with them in the Hunnic way", Octar said, and grinned. "They will know nothing of the presence of the Huns. Bradakos, do your duty to your king, and we will talk once you know what we are up against."

We rode out later that same afternoon with fifty men who were selected by Bradakos.

We were still far away from any Gothic activity and decided to eat well that evening. Once we entered enemy territory, we would have to sustain ourselves on cold rations. Lighting a campfire posed the risk of alerting the enemy to our presence.

Bradakos and I spent the evening devising a strategy to scout the area effectively. The fact that the scouts were familiar with the land would work in our favour.

Firstly we would set up a small, permanent camp about two days' ride in the direction of the foe. This camp would be manned by Bradakos and me, together with six warriors. Every day one of the riders would leave with an update to the king, returning four or five days later with any news from Apsikal.

The remainder would divide into four equal groups. Each group would fan out across the countryside and establish a temporary camp a day's ride away, in the direction of the Gothic advance. Each group of eleven scouts would split into three scouting parties of two riders each, with five men stationed at the camp. Two would always remain at the camp and three would ride to Bradakos and me with an information update.

This was the most efficient way to scout the largest area. Once our scouts had located the enemy, Bradakos and I would ride to investigate.

We spent the following morning relating the orders to the scouts and setting up structures of command. We scrutinized the gear of all to ensure that we had not left any small piece of metal uncovered. The easiest way for a scout to give away his position was for the sun to reflect off metal. Once we were satisfied, all the scouts verbally repeated their orders and eagerly set off to locate the enemy.

We dispatched a rider to the king to inform him that our scouting screen was in place and that we would keep him updated.

Sitting around and waiting for information to arrive is by far a more difficult task than gathering the information yourself, I realised. After sitting at the camp for three days, waiting for the feedback of the scouts, we decided to alter our routine.

To allay the boredom, Bradakos and I ventured out on short scouting patrols, leaving camp early in the morning and returning two watches later, normally just in time to receive the messengers from the outlying scouting groups.

I was no novice at scouting and had spent countless hours learning the tricks of the trade with the Roxolani scouts. I still believe the Huns are the best scouts in the world. I honed my skills during the year I spent with them.

When scouting in pairs, the riders would typically ride eighty paces apart. This would allow the riders to scan a greater area and not be influenced by the sounds of the other rider. Should one of the scouts fall prey to an ambush, the other has a chance to escape. Scouts communicate by means of hand signals and bird calls. Never, ever is talking allowed while scouting.

One morning, Bradakos was riding at the front, while I trailed about eighty paces behind. We followed a stream that meandered along a shallow gorge. The surrounding shrubs were dense, reaching up to the height of a man riding a tall horse.

I heard the bird call Bradakos used as a signal for me to approach. I spurred my horse into an easy trot and found Bradakos waiting for me in a clearing. He had dismounted and was sitting beside a stream in the shade of a small tree.

He indicated for me to join him.

"We have scouted this area for a week. There are none of the enemy in the vicinity", he said.

I went onto one knee and used my hand to scoop clear, cold water from the stream to wash my dusty face. I took a couple of swallows of the water as the day was getting hot and I was tired from the riding.

I tied my horse to a nearby shrub and allowed him enough leeway to quench his thirst.

Refreshed, I sat down next to Bradakos.

He drew a deep breath and I realised that there was something weighing heavily on his mind.

"Lucius", he said, and paused.

He never called me Lucius. Immediately he had my undivided attention.

"Lucius", he repeated, and said, "Before you and Nik arrived, I was next in line, after Apsikal, to rule the Roxolani."

"Apsikal was still grieving over the loss of his sons and he never broached the issue with me, but I knew it was inevitable for me to rule", Bradakos said.

"Then a young Roman boy arrived", he gave me half a smile, "and Apsikal asked me to train him."

"It was a risk, you know. I could have removed the obstacle that stood between me and the throne."

"The land of the Roxolani is very close to the land of the mighty Roman Empire. We have clashed with Rome many times in the past. We mostly lost. Apsikal is the reason that the Roxolani prospered until now, while other tribes have been ravaged and subdued by the terrible legions of the Empire. Apsikal spent years in Rome. He understands the Romans and he knows how to placate them and how to negotiate with them. But he is still a Scythian at heart, and also knows how to deal with brutal men like Octar. He saw in you the opportunity to have the best of both worlds. A son of a Roman nobleman to protect the tribe from the might of Rome, and the son of a Scythian princess that would be respected by the tribe and its allies."

"I had my doubts at first, but then something happened that annoyed me."

He shot me a quick grin, totally out of character for Bradakos. "To my surprise, I liked you. You had a will of iron. I nearly killed you with the training, but you endured against all odds. You are truly a Roxolani king at heart. I soon realised that you are gifted in other ways. I had to concentrate when sparring with you, else you would put me on my arse."

"That is why I followed you to the land of the Huns. I was curious as to how you would fare. Again, you won the respect of the Huns. That is not an easy thing to do, believe me."

He paused, as if contemplating to share something with me, but continued anyway. "Do you know the real reason why Octar wishes that I rule the Roxolani?" he asked. "I might be a warrior, but I understand the people of the Sea of Grass. Lucius, Octar is afraid of you. You are an enigma. Scythians are ruled by the strongest. He desires the Roxolani as part of the Hunnic confederation of tribes, where he is the strongest leader and the fiercest warrior. He sees in you the one who could surpass him and become the king of kings, the overlord. That is the real reason. The words will never be spoken by him, but believe me, I know."

I was speechless. My view of my own abilities was very different from Bradakos's.

Bradakos continued. "And then you challenged and defeated the Goth champion. Many warriors witnessed what you did. Do you realise what they are saying? The rumour is that you are the human incarnation of Arash, the god of war. No warrior, neither Roxolani nor Hun, would dare face you in combat. I, for one, would not, unless I wanted to die."

"I had given up the hope to be king long ago, but now I will do what I have to. For my people. I have realised that your destiny lies elsewhere. Where, I do not know, but you are too powerful for the Scythians. You will just end up destroying us, or destroying yourself."

"There, I have said what is in my heart", he sighed.

He stood, clasped my arm and then embraced me. "I would have followed you gladly, Lucius. You are more than a brother to me."

He walked away and mounted his horse. There was no more to be said.

The first rule of scouting on horseback is to acknowledge that your horse is able to smell and hear things that you can't. You have to be in tune with your animal and know him well enough to realise when he senses danger. As the big man rode away, my horse's ears pricked slightly. Just enough for me to take my strung bow from its case.

As I reached for the arrows in my side quiver, a bear burst from the thick shrubs right next to Bradakos. It was an enormous beast, matching the size of Bradakos's horse. The bear stood on its hind legs and slapped the terrified horse with a huge paw. The rearing horse lost its footing and fell, pinning Bradakos's leg underneath.

Before the beast could reach my mentor, five armour-piercing arrows slammed into its skull. It stood swaying from side to side above Bradakos as I skewered it through the heart with my two-handed spear, delivered at full gallop.

I turned my horse back towards Bradakos, who had crawled out from underneath his horse, apparently uninjured, but shaken nonetheless.

I dismounted, passed my wineskin to Bradakos, and said, "I enjoyed that. We must go hunting more often."

He scowled in reply.

Chapter 32 – Plan

Bradakos insisted on skinning the bear. "It is a good omen, given to you by Arash", he said. "We will take the skin. Do not shun a gift from the hands of the gods."

We arrived at the camp at the same time as the messenger. He was visibly keen to deliver his news and I immediately knew that our scouts had located the Goths. His words came out as a hoarse whisper and I stopped him with an upheld palm. I handed him my wineskin and motioned for him to drink. He drank deeply.

He nodded in appreciation, drew breath, and said, "We have located the enemy about eighty miles to the northeast. The Goths command an enormous army. The Carpi and other tribes have joined with their overlords. We estimate their numbers to be close to sixty thousand warriors."

Bradakos fiddled with the braids in his beard. "Tonight we rest", he said. "Tomorrow we leave before daybreak."

Bradakos had spoken much during the day. He was normally a man of few words. So, having exhausted his quota, we sat beside the fire and said little. We retired to the furs early, yet I slept fitfully, plagued by strange dreams of bears and huge armies. Nik always said that if you gorge on meat before you go to bed you end up with haunting nightmares.

I woke up tired. We took a bag filled with cold fare and set off with the scout leading the way. Late that afternoon we reached the camp of the scouts. It was too late to try and find the Goths, so we decided to ride out the following morning. Two scouts were shadowing the Gothic army and would alert us if they deviated from their course, or if anything untoward happened.

A scout woke us early, but I felt well rested. We finished the last of the leftover bear meat and washed it down with wine. A good start to the day.

The scout did a proper job. We travelled through small valleys, streams and gorges, always keeping to the low-lying areas.

Once or twice we were led into dense shrubs to allow enemy outriders to pass. We were travelling along a narrow valley when we heard the bird call issued by one of the shadowing scouts. As if by magic two of them appeared from a copse of small trees along a bend in the gorge. We did not talk. They motioned for us to dismount and lead our horses into the trees. The horses remained with one of them while another warrior led us to a rocky hill bordering the trees. We skirted the outcrop and crawled the last few paces to the boulder-strewn area that was the top of the ridge. It proved to be an excellent vantage point.

Below us lay a broad valley with luscious grass stretching to the horizon. A stream bordered the near side of the valley, providing water to the host spread out before us. And what a host it was. Thousands upon thousands of people, horses and wagons, as far as the eye could see.

An enemy host as vast as the one we witnessed immediately induces a feeling of panic. As if one has to defeat the army all on one's own. I had to breathe deeply for a few heartbeats to calm myself. To my surprise, there were many, many warriors that were riding horses. After our initial clashes with the Goths I expected mainly infantry. I had been wrong. At least fifteen thousand of the army consisted of light cavalry, with the rest being heavily armoured infantry.

Nik and I had studied many Roman scrolls on warfare. Most of them touch on how to estimate the size of an enemy marching in disorganised ranks. At this I was no expert. My estimates ranged from forty thousand to sixty thousand. Fortunately we had Bradakos and the scouts.

Once we had retreated and retrieved the horses, we conferred in whispers and agreed on a figure of fifteen thousand cavalry and thirty-five thousand footmen. The cavalry used shields, but they were generally not well armoured. Most were armed with javelins, but few had bows.

The scouts guided us safely out of the enemy territory, masterfully dodging the outriders of the foe.

We recalled the scouts from the outlying camps, but left a few men to keep an eye on the advancing Goths.

We rode back to the kings, making haste.

En route to the camp I tried to imagine how the battle would unfold. Would there be a plan, a strategy, or would the armies just have a go at each other, the barbarian way?

The major weakness of the barbarians was, surprisingly, the lack of any written military history. It meant that the same mistakes could be repeated, century after century, battle after battle.

This weakness did not exist in the Roman world. Rome's historians detailed the battles where Rome emerged victorious and stated the reasons why they had triumphed. Even more effort was spent on analysing major defeats. Nik and I had studied and discussed all these in detail during my years of tutoring.

I knew what had to be done. The Gothic cavalry had to be removed from the battle as quickly as possible. Then the Roxolani and the Huns could destroy the enemy infantry at their leisure. How could I influence this? I came up with a plan.

The first part of my strategy involved Bradakos.

While riding beside him, I said, "Bradakos, I have never requested a favour from you. May I do so now?"

He looked at me with a frown on his face.

"I am not setting a trap for you, Bradakos, I desire only for the Goths to be defeated", I said.

"Tell me your plan, I will help you." Bradakos said. "I am one of those who believe that the god of war whispers into your ear."

Maybe he was right.

I shared my plan with Bradakos.

Soon after we arrived back at the main camp, Bradakos reported to the kings. I slipped away to find Gordas.

"Eochar, I heard that you have located the enemy. My men are hungry for scalps and plunder. When do we ride?" the Hun said.

I took Gordas aside and said, "Gordas, I had never asked you for a favour. May I do so now?" I received the same reaction as with Bradakos, but he agreed.

I went to visit my father and explained to him what I wished to achieve.

"I like your plan. The Gothic cavalry needs to be dealt with, I agree. I will speak with Apsikal."

The most dangerous part of my plan needed to be put in place. I went to speak with the great man. The king of the Huns.

Gordas arranged it for me. I entered the tent and went down on one knee. The Hun king did not raise me to my feet, but left me there to tell my story. I made a deal to save my people, to save everyone, and to defeat the Goths. I spoke frankly to the king. Too frankly. There was always a risk that he would have his bodyguards run me through, but nothing worthwhile is accomplished without risk.

By the time the sun set, all had been arranged. I sat down with Nik beside the fire and asked for wine. I drank deeply and asked for a refill. He complied.

I went to bed with mixed feelings. I knew that we could defeat the Goths and save my people, but the price that it demanded weighed heavily on my mind.

Chapter 33 – Day of reckoning

I leaned forward in the saddle and stroked the neck of my favourite Hunnic horse. I had formed a tight bond with him over the years. He was named Şimşek, or Lightning, due to the contrasting white mark on his forehead.

My hand rested on his neck and I felt his apprehension. The same tension that was coursing through my veins.

To my right, a broad valley stretched to the horizon. A rocky hill, acting as my vantage point, split the valley into a fork of two narrower valleys, diverging at an angle. The narrower valley to the south, where the Goths were amassing, was ideally suited to them. They could secure both their left and right wing without fear of being flanked by the mobile Scythians, who possessed cavalry only. I watched as the thousands upon thousands of warriors deployed for battle, wading through the thin morning fog. Their armour glinted dully in the dim early-morning light while the whetted blades of their grounded spears caught the first rays of the rising sun.

They deployed with a frontage of more than a mile, twenty men deep - their line thick, strong and unbreakable. Their left flank was protected by my low rock-strewn hill. On their right flank, I noticed the cavalry. A brightly coloured, milling mass of Goths and assimilated Scythian and Germanic horsemen.

On the far side of the enemy cavalry, a deep river gorge protected them from being outflanked by the Roxolani horsemen.

The numbers of the Roxolani and the Huns appeared meagre against the overwhelming horde of the Goths.

There was little order to the Roxolani's cavalry. The centre and right consisted of twenty thousand Huns, all mounted, of course. On the left flank, three thousand Roxolani light cavalry could be differentiated. Ten paces behind the horde, two thousand heavy horsemen were patiently waiting in perfectly dressed ranks.

The Goths outnumbered us two to one. I studied the scene from my vantage point, high up on the ridge of the hill which anchored the left flank of the enemy. I watched in silence as a Hun dragged the scalped corpse of another Goth scout into the cover of nearby shrubs.

Fifteen miles farther along the northern fork of the valley, Gordas and his warband waited on my signal.

I guided Şimşek down the slope on the far side of the hill to ensure that I would remain unseen. Then I raised my spear to which a piece of white linen was tied.

The die was cast.

On my signal, Gordas led his men down the fork of the valley towards my position. They would have to travel at least fifteen miles. Within sixty heartbeats, an immense cloud of dust rose on the horizon. Shortly after, the commanders of the Gothic army pointed in the direction of the dust. They dispatched a rider to scout out the northern fork of the valley. He investigated and raced his horse back to report. The dust cloud was enormous, created by Gordas and his men. The horses were pulling branches which were tied to the saddles, creating a dust cloud that would be attributed to a much larger host than a mere thousand riders.

The moment of truth had arrived. I could see the Gothic commanders deliberating. Moments later, at least ten thousand of the Goth horsemen detached from the right flank of the enemy to engage the approaching threat.

Gordas and his men reined in when they detected the approaching Goth cavalry. They formed a front with their left flank against the slope of my hill, and their right flank unprotected. To the rear of the Hun horsemen, two thousand heavily armoured Roxolani riders readied themselves. They were screened from the Goths by the Hun cavalry.

Three thousand men cannot stand against ten thousand, especially when they can be flanked and enveloped.

The Goths realised the opportunity, and half of their cavalry split off, accelerating to hit the Huns in the right flank. The Goths were no fools and slowed down their frontal charge to allow their flanking manoeuvre to hit the Huns at the same time. The Huns milled around undecided while the thousands of Goths thundered down upon them. The Huns seemed to wake from their slumber and started to pour thousands of arrows into the Goths executing the frontal attack. The loose formation of the Huns then parted as the heavily armoured horses accelerated through gaps in the line.

But the charge of the Goths aimed at the right flank would annihilate the Huns, who seemed to be unaware of the danger. The Roxolani heavy cavalry burst through the open formation of the Huns and bore down on the charging Goths. The Scythians carried no shields, but were armoured from head to toe in heavy scale and chain, rendering them nearly immune to arrows and javelins. Their horses were similarly armoured.

At forty paces apart the Goths hurled their deadly light javelins into the ranks of the cataphracts, immediately followed by a second volley. The weapons that would normally devastate a light cavalry charge, had minimal effect on the cataphracts, the javelins harmlessly deflecting off the heavy scales and chain.

There was an audible clash when the Goths were hit by the huge armoured horses and the heavy two-handed spears. At least two thousand Goths died in less than a heartbeat.

The flanking Goths stretched out in a long line and held their javelins ready to pour into the Huns. Just before they released, their charge faltered as thousands of horses stumbled or fell as if the invisible hand of a god had hit them from above. The horses in the second and third ranks were unable to stop and careened into the fallen animals and riders, killing and maiming hundreds.

In the timespan of a few heartbeats the Goths were reduced by half. The remaining riders panicked, and their commanders led them back down the valley to join their infantry, only to find their path blocked by thousands of howling Huns. Six thousand surviving Goths were caught between the terrible Hun warband and the regrouping cataphracts of the Roxolani. The only option left for them was to die bravely.

I had gambled all on the strategy to remove the cavalry of the Goths. Octar exacted a heavy price in return for giving me command of the five thousand Huns who cut off the retreat of the Goths. The Huns had no other option but to ride thirty miles to circle around the unsuspecting Goths. They entered the valley from the north, under cover of darkness, and waited until the Goths were committed to the charge before racing to cut off the retreat.

Our flank that seemed vulnerable was protected by sixty thousand leg-breaker holes, dug the day before by the Huns. At first, when I made the suggestion, they refused, threatening violence. Fortunately, Bradakos had been right about many things. I threw down the gauntlet to men who refused me. No one wished to face the human incarnation of Arash in battle, so the holes were dug and camouflaged.

The loss of the majority of their cavalry caused the Goths to hesitate. They were reluctant to engage.

The Roxolani cavalry regrouped and rounded the base of the hill, intent on striking the unprotected rear of the Gothic infantry, with my band of six thousand Huns hot on their heels.

Seeing the Roxolani approach, the main Hun army initiated their attack. Thousands of seemingly disorganized riders fell into line and accelerated until they rode at blistering speed in a whirlwind of dust and horses.

The remaining Goth cavalry tried bravely to protect the rear of their infantry from the Roxolani heavy cataphracts. But they were overrun by a wall of iron, their bodies trampled. With the cataphracts' horses spent, my Huns fell on the rear of the enemy infantry, devastating their ranks. The Goths with the weakest armour and the least experience stood at the rear of the formation. They were the ones who Gordas's Huns engaged. Armour-piercing arrows, filed to a needle point, were released from the powerful horn bows at short range, felling thousands of Goths.

The front ranks of the Goths were filled with hardened veterans. The bravest of the brave, proven in battle. With their thick shields they waited patiently, ready to endure the onslaught.

But no one could stand against the arrow storm that followed. All shafts were concentrated along a hundred-pace section, right in the centre of the line. Thousands upon thousands of arrows finding the smallest of weaknesses in their armour or the smallest gaps between shields. When the front ranks inevitably faltered, a thousand of the Roxolani cataphracts split the enemy formation in two, riding boot to boot, fifty riders wide and twenty deep - an unstoppable force of flesh and metal that sliced through the Gothic ranks like a hot dagger through butter.

The Goths broke. Just like that. Assailed from all sides, they fled, trying to reach the gorge on the right flank. Some sections tried to retreat in good order, others gave up their lives to allow their comrades to reach safety, but most just abandoned their weapons and ran away.

The Huns killed thousands, shooting fleeing warriors in the back at point-blank range. Others they snared with their terrible lassos, dragging them through the dust, or leaning down from the saddle and striking with the deadly Hunnic axe. The rout became a slaughter.

Chapter 34 – Aftermath

The women and children of the Goths did not accompany their husbands and fathers. Although I loathed the Goths, I did not wish to see the Huns unleashed on innocents. Thousands of the Goths escaped the slaughter, but at least half of the enemy perished on the field of battle.

I noticed that Octar's men had rounded up two hundred captives. No doubt they had a horrific fate in mind for those poor souls, else they would have just killed them outright.

The Huns were ecstatic. Taking scalps, looting swords, armour and anything else of value. They would leave the field rich with booty. The horses that survived were rounded up and saddled. Looted gear was meticulously loaded onto wagons. Only corpses and unwanted clothes would remain once the victors abandoned the field.

I roamed the battlefield aimlessly, trying not to feel guilty about how effective my plan had been.

I remember stumbling upon Gordas.

"I see Arash is admiring the fruits of his labour", he said with a grin. "The warriors are chanting your name, my friend. Some thought you were the terrible god of war incarnate, now they have seen it with their own eyes and they truly believe it. Shit, even I think so."

The big man slapped me on the back with a paw. "We will feast tonight. First, we gather the spoils before the stench of death draws the flies and the vermin. I will see you tonight."

As he rode away, I noticed bright blood dripping from the dozens of scalps adorning his saddle. The flanks of his horse were stained red from the gory harvest.

Back at the camp I found Nik and Cai beside the campfire, sharing wine. I had not disclosed all the details of the plan I had concocted. Nik came to his feet and embraced me. "You have done well, my son. The camp is filled with tales of your success." I smiled wearily and joined them. Cai passed me a cup of wine.

It is not in my nature to brood on things, so I jumped right in. "There was no way that we could have defeated the Gothic cavalry without the help of the five thousand Huns."

Nik and Cai nodded in agreement and waited for me to continue.

"Octar would never have let me take command of a portion of his men without expecting something significant in return", I sighed. "My people, the Roxolani, had to survive. I could not stand idly by while my people are slaughtered in a pitched battle when outnumbered two to one. And I had a strategy that I believed in."

"People see you as hero, one who deliver them from brink of destruction", Cai said. "Keep plan secret is good. Wise general said plan must be impenetrable as night, and if move, fall like thunderbolt. He be proud as I."

"I knew what Octar desired, so I paid him a visit and traded the thing he wanted most, for temporary command of his men", I replied.

Cai frowned. I think he suspected that I might have given my jian sword to Octar. Nik just wore a general confused look.

"My martial success, combined with my noble birth, is a growing threat to Octar, especially with the Roxolani being allied to the Huns in future", I said. "I made an oath that I would leave the territory of the Scythians and return to the lands of my youth, to the Roman Empire."

Cai and Nik were stunned into silence. They just looked at me and drank deeply from their cups.

Nik smiled and said, "You have the heart of a warrior, but even better, the ingenuity of a true Roman. My time to cross the river is approaching, I can feel it in my bones. I have been yearning to go back to Sirmium, but I wished to stay here, to see you become the king of the tribe. I will gladly accompany you back to our home. The gods work in mysterious ways, my son."

I was unsure if I could broach the subject of Nik being a wanted man in Rome. I trusted Cai, but I said nothing. Nik picked up on my hesitation and said, "I have spent many days in the company of Cai. He cares for you nearly as much as I do. I have told Cai about how we came to live with the Roxolani. Feel free to speak openly."

"Nik, how is it that you do not fear going back to Sirmium? We are wanted men."

Nik stared into the fire, as if to recall details from long before. "There was a name at the top of Commodus's death list. That name I have never mentioned. He is the man who wished the evidence removed to protect himself and to protect his descendants. It is Septimius Severus, who became emperor a year after Commodus was killed. He was the man who paid the gold for the death of Commodus. He was the man who signed my letter. The emperors who succeeded Commodus were a farce, all planned by Septimius. He was a hard man, a soldier, and he ruled with a fist of iron for nearly twenty years. When we fled Sirmium, Septimius had died already, but it was the grandmother of the boy emperor, Severus Alexander, who had wanted us dead. She was the sister of Septimius's wife, and part of the conspiracy. She and her witch of a daughter,

Julia Mamaea, made sure that I would never set foot in Roman lands again."

"But the gods had other plans. Julia Mamaea and her son, Severus Alexander, were killed on the order of Maximinus Thrax, the new emperor, but a few months ago in Mogantiacum."

The old man had tears in his eyes when he looked up from the fire. "Lucius, the last of the descendants of Septimius Severus is dead. We can go home. Even to Rome if we really wanted to. We are free, thank the gods."

Cai placed his arm around Nik. "I go with you, my friend. I tied to Lucius by destiny, foretold by master of Dao. I go where he go, and journey getting interesting."

As Cai finished speaking, Bradakos strolled in.

"Lucius, the warriors are asking for you. You have won great fame. With you as the general of the Roxolani, no enemy will be able to stand against us."

I felt bad to upset him on such a day filled with victory, but I told him the tale of the deal I had made with Octar.

"Bradakos, it was the only way", I said when I was done. "The Goths will not dare bother us for many years to come. The Roxolani will be safe within their new alliance."

Chapter 35 – Feast

The feast was a lavish affair. Only the nobles of the Huns and the Roxolani were invited, the common warriors feasted on horsemeat and got drunk on looted Gothic beer and mead.

Nik and Cai also joined us, and of course Bradakos had to be there as the heir apparent.

Fires were lit underneath huge copper cauldrons filled with all kinds of meat. Beef, mutton, horse, venison and fowl. Whole oxen and sheep roasted over open fires.

We ate cheese, looted from the Goths, and enjoyed fine red wine. I sat in the company of my friends. Bradakos occupied the seat of honour on the right of Apsikal, not far from where we were sitting.

I enjoyed the wine, but I did not overdo it. Savouring it, rather than swallowing it down as fast as possible. Before everyone was too drunk to focus, Apsikal stood to say words.

The chatter stopped immediately. Apsikal looked around the quiet host and said, "Today we have sealed the friendship of the Huns and the Roxolani in the blood of our enemies. We have avenged the warriors who died at the hands of the oathbreakers. The Roxolani will rise again."

He pumped his fist in the air and the warriors erupted in loud cheering and howling. He waited for the cheering to subside and continued. "King Octar and I have strengthened the alliance between our peoples, we have formed an alliance that will see our enemies cowered."

Predictably, cheering erupted.

Apsikal sat down, basking in the admiration of his people. Octar, the mighty high king of the Huns, stood. "The enemy of the Roxolani will be the enemy of the Hun, and the enemy of the Hun will be the enemy of the Roxolani. We have seen today that not even the mighty army of the Goths could stand against the combined power of our warriors. We will be invincible."

I thought that the cheering couldn't be any louder, but I was wrong. This time it was.

"Eochar, the brave nephew of King Apsikal, devised a plan that is worthy of Arash", Octar said, and waved me to my feet.

As I had rehearsed with Octar, I heaped praise upon him, to the loud cheering and howling of the Huns. Grinning, Octar acknowledged my words with a nearly imperceptible nod.

When all had calmed down, I said, "I heard that there is a rumour that my path is directed by Arash." Silence fell on the gathering, as all wanted to hear of my interaction with the gods.

"That is true, Arash has spoken to me." There was a loud intake of breath as the speculation was confirmed. People started to converse in whispers. I held up my hand to silence them.

"I have received direction from Arash in a dream. In the middle of the night, he came to me and gave me instructions." Total silence ensued. I had their full attention, even the drunk ones.

"He told me that my destiny lies not with the Huns, but that I must travel back to the land of my birth." There was another collective intake of breath.

"Arash has a task for me, but it is in the land of the Romans. Only a complete fool would ignore the command of the god of war." All around, I could see heads nodding in agreement.

"And I am no fool. I will heed the command of Arash so that it may go well with his people, the Huns and the Roxolani."

I sat down.

Octar gestured for me to approach. He stood and embraced me like a brother, to the adoring howls and cheers of the nobles. "Nicely done, Eochar. That was even better than I had expected", he whispered.

Only Nik, Cai and Bradakos knew that I was telling the truth.

* * *

Bradakos had explained the situation to Apsikal. He was saddened when he found out that we would be departing soon. He realised that I had played a major role in the victory over the Goths and ultimately saving our people. He wished to reward me with gold, but I refused.

Octar was never the trusting type. He remained with his army to see me off. He obviously wanted to make sure I stayed true to my word. Better safe than sorry, eh?

Bradakos arranged for a group of fifty Roxolani warriors to escort us to the northern bank of the Danube. We transported all our belongings on packhorses with no carts to slow us down. A small herd of Hunnic mounts accompanied us. Octar had gifted me a number of horses and in addition I had purchased more of the hardy animals from the herd of the king.

We were all packed and ready to leave when Bradakos arrived, leading two packhorses, encumbered with heavy leather bags. "Octar asked me to give you this", he said. "The Hun king said that it was the final part of your deal."

I walked over to the horse and opened the bag for Bradakos to take a peek. The bags were filled with gold coins. Thousands.

"I fight like a Roxolani, but I negotiate like a Roman", I said, and grinned.

With that I jumped on my Hun horse and rode away, leaving a speechless Bradakos in my dust.

Chapter 36 – Goodbye Bradakos

We made good time on our return trip to the Empire. Not for one moment did I fret about our safety or worry about the coinage. Fifty heavily armed Roxolani, led by Bradakos, were more than enough to scare away any bandit rabble.

Eventually we reached the Yazyges village on the barbarian side of the Danube. Little had changed since I had last visited. There were clearly two groups of people - Romanised barbarians, and barbarianised Romans. It was difficult to establish from which group an individual hailed until he spoke.

It was still early in the afternoon when we set up camp on the outskirts of the village. Nik called me over and we paid a visit to the nearby stream to rid ourselves of the dust, sweat and grime of the last couple of days in the saddle. Refreshed, and having donned clean clothes, I joined the warriors at the cooking fire. I resembled a typical barbarian. The wild, uncivilized type. My long hair was plated in a variety of braids and my beard was prominent, although not yet thick and full. I wore the typical multi-coloured, loose-fitting clothing worn by the Scythians.

Nik approached me with what looked like a knife in his hand. On closer inspection I realised it was by far a more intimidating weapon - a pair of scissors. I tried to protest, but

Nik would have none of it, to the great amusement of my Roxolani friends.

Nik cut my hair short, in the style of the time. To my horror, he also wielded a razor and oil, and proceeded to shave my beard.

Once he was done, he produced a brand-new set of clothes - a new linen tunic and an expensive-feeling, thick, woollen cloak, complete with a set of sandals. Nik stepped back to admire his work and I made a comment of sorts, in Scythian, of course.

"Lucius, when in Rome, do as the Romans do. Once we have crossed the river, we will speak in Latin only", Nik said.

Bradakos approached us, returning from some activity or other, scowled, and addressed Nik in Scythian, his hand going to the hilt of his sword.

"Is there a problem….", he started.

That was as far as he got when recognition dawned on him. "I'll be damned", was all he could utter as he walked away, shaking his head.

To Nik's amusement, I changed back into my barbarian clothes to spend the evening as a Scythian with Bradakos and the Roxolani warriors.

We drank good Roman red wine and consumed loads of cheese, olives and other Roman delicacies which Nik had procured in the village. It felt strange to feast on Roman food in the company of the Roxolani. It was an evening to remember. Bradakos temporarily packed away his scowl and we had good laughs as we reminisced about the six years I had spent east of the Danube.

The following morning we did not rise as early as usual. There was no rush, as we were only a mile or two from the river crossing at Viminacium.

The Roxolani spent their time preparing for the trip back home. Nik had procured ample quantities of all kinds of food for their journey.

Bradakos strode in our direction, leading his packhorse. I ambled in the direction of the mules and gestured for him to join me. I handed him a heavy saddlebag. He took it from me, frowning.

"This is a small gesture of appreciation", I said. "You will find two thousand gold coins in there." He moved to hand the bag back to me, but by then I had Bradakos's measure.

"I have never refused the gifts you offered me", I said. "Countless hours of effort to turn me into a warrior, protecting me, making sure that I would survive. Now I offer you a simple gift. Would you refuse and insult me?"

Bradakos dropped his gaze, defeated, and clasped my arm, holding on to the bag.

He held my arm in a vice like grip, not realising his strength. "Before we left on the return trip, I had asked for ten volunteers from the ranks of the Roxolani warriors."

Now he had me interested.

He realised he was still gripping my arm and released it. He smiled and fixed me with a sidelong glance. "Nik told me that you wish to breed horses. These warriors will assist you to get your farm up and running. They will stay for a year. They are knowledgeable and hardworking. All I ask in return is that you reward them fairly, even though they are happy to do it for free."

"Thank you, brother, I accept", I replied.

Chapter 37 – Crossing the Danube

We arrived on the northern bank of the river in less than a watch. The Roman bank of the Danube was obscured by a grey, wet, fog that melted into the dark water.

We had said our goodbyes, turning my mood as dark as the ominous-looking river. I was already regretting leaving the wild lands of the Scythian people. People with little reason to lie and deceive.

I trailed behind Nik, who headed straight for a sizeable barge suitable for ferrying men and supplies across the river. I took the ferryman for a barbarian, but Nik addressed him in Latin and he replied in the tongue of the Romans.

Our garb and accents identified us as wealthy Roman traders. The ferryman assumed that we were knowledgeable about the prevailing rates and we settled on two gold coins. Late afternoon, after traversing the river several times, the last of our party arrived on the Roman side of the river. Two Roman men, one man from the mystical land of Serica, ten mounted barbarian warriors, and thirty Hunnic horses. Not to mention five thousand gold coins.

Once you cross the river, you still have to get inside the wall. There had been no uprising or invasion for years, which explained the relaxed attitude of the Roman soldiers. With our perfect Latin and expensive clothes, we were not afforded a second glance. A duty centurion did consider searching our baggage after making eye contact with our Roxolani guards, but two gold coins later we were on our way.

We reversed the route that we had travelled under duress many years before, making our way to Singidunum on the broad and well-kept Via Militaris. Our Roxolani guards stared wide-eyed, as they had never laid eyes on a road constructed in the Roman fashion. Large blocks of stone had been used to build this eight-pace-wide wonder. It was made to withstand heavy military traffic and to facilitate lightning fast deployment of thousands of infantry and cavalry.

We encountered countless merchants and travellers, their stares lingering on Cai and eventually on the Roxolani, causing them time and again to lower their eyes to avoid a possible confrontation. I soon realised that it had become a game for my barbarians to intimidate oncoming traffic. I intervened and asked them not to scare the nice people. None of the warriors gainsaid me. They all believed that I was either Arash incarnate, or the messenger of the god.

I was not entirely blameless for encouraging that belief. I rode close to the warriors, then mumbled as if conversing with an imaginary entity. When I knew I had their attention, I rolled my eyes upward, as if looking into my skull. Afterwards I turned to meet their gaze with only the whites of my eyes showing, muttering unintelligibly.

I noticed Cai looking at me, scowling and shaking his head, seeing straight through my ruse.

Our guards did not lack courage. My barbarians would charge a foe of overwhelming odds without fear of death, but one look at my little ruse left them wide-eyed with fear. People are funny that way.

Anyway, it served its purpose. The warriors actually waved and smiled at the next group of surprised merchants, who waved and smiled back, probably inspired more by fear than friendliness.

We didn't try to reach Singidunum that evening. Unleashing the Roxolani in the town would have seen us all end up in jail. We made camp late in the afternoon, ten miles outside the settlement.

We lit a fire and gorged on the delicious provisions that Nik had procured. There was no need for rationing as we would be home in a day or two. I favoured the rich cheeses and olives and washed it down with big gulps of red wine.

I was tired, sad to leave my old life behind, but also filled with anticipation. Sleep came easily as the Roxolani had informed me that they would take care of sentry duties that evening.

Maybe it had something to do with my little trick during the day?

I was riding on Şimşek. We travelled at speed, flying across the landscape. Leading the way was a huge warrior on a massive, powerful horse, fully armed and armoured, his mount bristling with scale and chain.

We rode past warbands of Huns, unnoticed. We flashed past the tented camp of the Roxolani, constantly gathering speed, our horses only gaining strength, with no sign of tiring.

My companion reined in when we reached the mighty Danube. He shot me a sidelong glance and I could see that it was no man. His blue eyes shone with the brightness of the sun. The massive muscles of his arms bulging, his hand resting on the silver pommel of his sword.

He extended his arm and pointed a finger to the lands of Rome. He looked at me again, and suddenly I understood. He slapped my horse on the rump and it walked into the river.

I did not look back - the war god had spoken.

I never again repeated the joke I had played on the Roxolani guards.

Chapter 38 – Sirmium

Cai waited outside the gates of Sirmium to babysit the Roxolani.

Nik and I rode straight to the offices of the procurator. We decided that the best strategy would be to grab the bull by the horns. Nik would confront the man who sold us out. He would have no further reason to betray us, as his master had died.

Half a dozen legionaries were guarding the offices of the representative of the emperor. We approached a legionary and I said, "Please tell us if Sextus Quintilius Condianus is in attendance."

He looked me up and down and a smirk appeared on his face. "You're not going to find him here, are you? Better go look in the cemetery, it's that way", he said, and chuckled at his own jest.

Nik handed me a copy of the document that the procurator had signed all those years ago.

I presented the guard with the scroll, the imperial seal of the procurator clearly visible. "I have business to attend to at the office of the new procurator", I said, and watched the smirk disappear from his face, now concerned that he might have offended someone of importance.

"Allow me to show you inside, good sir", was the best recovery he could muster, and led us along a tiled portico.

We knocked on the door of the office of the clerk to the procurator, and entered. To our surprise, it was still the same little Greek. He did not look up from his desk, but said, "Yes?"

Nik smiled at me and replied, "Tell your master that the Olympian has arrived."

The Greek secretary's head jerked up as he scrutinized us. Recognition dawned and he turned as white as his bleached tunic, which is no small feat for a Greek. He swallowed slowly, wiping his sweaty hands on his tunic underneath the table.

"I meant, may I be of assistance?" he said, and forced a smile.

I showed him the rental agreement we had with the state of Pannonia Inferior. He nodded and walked out a back door of his office, only to appear a couple of heartbeats later with a purse and a sealed letter.

The clerk leaned towards us and proceeded to speak in a conspiratorial whisper. "Sextus Condianus was a good friend of mine. He trusted me. When the cavalry that was supposed to apprehend you never reported back, he knew they would come for him." He leaned back and added, almost as if speaking only to himself, "They don't tolerate failure."

He snapped back to the present. "The governor said it had to do with the emperor and that my life would be forfeit if I knew the details. I requested him not to tell me. A month later they came for him, but officially he killed himself. He did have time to give me this, though", he said, and handed me a purse and a letter.

Nik took the purse, looked inside, and counted out sixteen gold aurei, representing more than a year's pay for the Greek.

Nik stacked the coins on the desk in two towers of equal height. He slid eight coins across the desk. "This is for what you have done", he said, and passed the other coins to the clerk in the same manner. "And this is for your help in future."

The Greek stared at the piles of coins for a span of heartbeats, like a man who had already decided to take the bribe, only taking time to convince himself that it was the correct choice.

He swept the coins off the table and scooped them into his open left hand while nodding with resigned acceptance.

Nik didn't open the letter. He handed me the remainder of the coins, but I waved it away.

"Nik, I have five thousand gold coins given to me by Octar, why would I need fifty more?"

We found Cai and the warriors where we left them. Nik opened the purse and gave each of the Roxolani two gold coins, explaining that it was their pay for the next three months, given in advance. It took two weeks for them to stop smiling.

We found the farm in more or less the same state that we had left it. Vagrants had made the deserted barn their home, but fled, leaving all behind, once they caught a glimpse of the barbarian warriors.

Come evening we had ourselves a feast. We had purchased two sheep from a farmer on his way to the market, and Nik and I had procured cheese, red wine and olives. To top it all, we managed to lay our hands on a large bag of freshly baked loaves of bread.

Soon the warriors had the sheep spitted over a fire, while I assisted Nik and Cai with the difficult task of sampling the amphora of wine and munching on the delicious cheese.

Even though I had no long-term plan, I knew what I wanted to achieve with the farm, but I had no idea of how I would go about it.

I decided to broach the subject with Nik and Cai.

"Nik, I would like you and Cai to help me build a villa", I said. "It will have to be more of a fortified compound than a villa. Could you do that?"

Nik regarded me with raised eyebrows. "I assume that you have afforded this topic some thought?" he said.

I nodded and continued. "Cai, I am sure that Nik told you that we had been attacked on this farm many years ago. I would not want to suffer a repeat of that incident. We were unprepared. Maybe we have no enemies at the gates at the moment, but things change. We are close to the *limes*, the border-fortifications of the Danube. Who knows when the Goths will come?"

Nik winked. "I agree, Lucius. Tell me what plan you and Arash have been concocting."

"Ideally I want a stone-walled compound, one hundred paces square, with two gates and towers at the gates, protected by a ditch, and the wall defended by an inner walkway", I said. "But we have not enough men to patrol four hundred paces of walls, so fifty paces square would have to do. Dressed stone of the quality we require is very expensive and we would draw the gaze of the procurator should we build in stone. A sturdy wooden palisade would have to suffice. We lack men to guard two gates, so we make do with one. We will construct a ditch, fifteen feet deep, and use the spoils as a base for the wooden palisades."

I winked at them. "I also have another idea, but that is my secret for the time being. Let's call it a surprise from Arash."

Nik and Cai were a wealth of knowledge. Cai sketched plans for the complex. To my surprise he was adroit at designing, and soon we had a detailed drawing of a fortified villa.

Calculating the quantities of materials required proved to be a challenge, but within a few weeks we had a detailed list of supplies needed to construct our new home.

We had to travel to Sirmium to procure, and place orders, for the necessary materials.

In order to get the job done as efficiently as possible, we split up, with Nik and Cai operating as a team, as Cai did not have full command of Latin as yet.

I had a list of items to arrange, and my first stop was the office of the secretary to the procurator.

The little Greek was named Alexander, believe it or not. I met with Alexander and explained our need for the services of a master builder. The Greeks in the area was a close-knit community, and he recommended a builder called Apolodorus.

Apolodorus was a master builder, specialising in wooden constructions. He had a team of twenty-five labourers who worked on projects in and around Sirmium. As he was available and without current commitments, I met him later that afternoon at the office of Alexander. The builder was quite a character, and obviously knew his trade. We soon reached an agreement and clasped forearms before going our separate ways.

I had arranged with Nik and Cai to stay over in Sirmium until we had obtained all the necessary labour and materials for the project. Nik volunteered to arrange the lodgings and it did not disappoint. He secured accommodation at an upmarket inn where each of us had our own room. As an added benefit, the inn was equipped with private baths. Late afternoon we washed off the sweat and dust of the day while sharing our experiences. We treated ourselves to an early dinner of hearty beef stew accompanied by bread, cheese and olives. Satisfied, we retired for the evening.

On the morrow I left my room early and made my way to the kitchen where I exchanged two coppers for a glass of fresh goat milk and a handful of dried figs. I made my way across town to the slave market. It was not an auction day, so no slaves were on public display. Not that it mattered, because I had something very specific in mind.

The slave dealer was a man of unknown origin who spoke Latin with an accent I couldn't quite place, mainly due to his lisp. He had the dark hair, thick black beard and bearing of a

Thracian, but his eyes were that of a Scythian. Had I not spent time with the Huns, I would have described his whole demeanour as intimidating, but given my experiences, I was immune to his appearance. He was simply known as Blandus, which, ironically, meant "charming".

I explained my requirement to Blandus, who could barely contain his greedy excitement. When slaves are sold on order and not at an auction, as is the norm, the price is much higher. The sale of slaves at auctions is overseen by the local quaestor, but a private deal presented the trader with the opportunity to dodge the onerous taxes.

I left behind a smiling, waving Blandus a quarter of a watch later, albeit with a much lighter purse.

Cai and Nik allowed me my little game of secrecy and they did not enquire as to my whereabouts.

Within a week, Apolodorus arrived on the farm with his labourers and two heavy-duty wagons filled with tents, tools and supplies.

The first day was spent setting up a temporary work camp, which he set out meticulously. I immediately realised that Alexander had provided us with an artisan of quality.

Apolodorus spent the next day with us, setting out the foundations while giving advice based on the sun's position in summer and winter, the prevailing winds, and from which direction the rain would most likely fall. It eventually took us two days to chop and change, but all of us, including Apolodorus, were satisfied that we had optimised the design.

The digging of the trench and the construction of the rampart, using the spoils, started the following morning. I decided that I would not just watch, but participate, and work alongside the labourers.

I rose before sunrise every morning, and either trained with Cai at the sword, or practised my archery and riding skills with my barbarian warriors. After a big breakfast that typically included ham, bread, eggs and cheese, I joined the labourers in the ditch, which was not dug all in one go. We removed two feet of soil at a time and used poles with metal plates to compact the spoil into layers around the huge anchor posts dug into the virgin earth, on the inside of the ditch. We repeated this process until the V-shaped ditch was fifteen feet deep and the rampart of the same height, and with the anchor poles firmly embedded into the rampart. I dug earth and loaded it into huge baskets, hauled the baskets along to the required site, and dumped the spoil. I compacted the spoils on the rampart. Other days we carried the massive anchor poles on our blistered shoulders. I ate like a bear in the evenings - chunks of beef, cheese, dates and olives. All swallowed down with good red wine. Then I slept, only to repeat the process the next day.

Within a month I became extremely fit. The martial training, combined with the heavy labour, made me stronger and more muscular. I enjoyed it, and learned in the process.

Occasionally I reluctantly ventured into the city to purchase items that we did not have in stock on the farm.

We decided to have the gates manufactured in Sirmium, rather than at the farm, because of the special skills required to attach the metal strips tightly onto the wood of the gates. We spared no expense, but it did not matter, as I had more gold than I could ever spend.

Once the trench and palisades were erected, the work involved less labour and more expertise, especially the carpentry. I realised that I did not possess the necessary skills, and I shifted my focus to scout the countryside with Nik and Cai.

As the weather turned colder and the days became shorter, Apolodorus completed the project.

The palisade protected the main house, stables, stores, servant quarters as well as barracks for the guards.

Apolodorus delivered a product of quality, and I rewarded him with a bonus of ten gold coins.

That evening we celebrated the completion of the project. On the morning after, I woke up in my own room, on my new bed, where I had been carried to the previous evening. The last thing I could remember was singing and laughing with Apolodorus and the Roxolani. Wine.

While I was lying in bed, enjoying the privacy, I reflected. I was the owner of a farm complete with an impressive villa, at least fifty of some of the most exotic horses in the world, and I had more gold than I could ever spend.

But yet, I realised that all was not well with me. It was like a scratch on the inside of my skull, a growing discontentment. It did not make sense. I had everything I could desire, and yet…

Chapter 39 – Tribune

Blandus dispatched a message from Sirmium informing me that my special order of slaves had arrived.

Leaving early in the morning, I rode to Sirmium with four of my barbarian guards to collect my newly acquired property.

The Dacians were all muscular men with long, blonde hair. Not that much different from my Roxolani guards.

Once we had waved goodbye to an ecstatic Blandus, we left Sirmium and took the road to the farm.

I had brought horses for the slaves, but they were still in chains, which made riding difficult. We rode in silence for ten miles and dismounted next to a stream to water the horses.

On my instruction the guards assisted the Dacians to dismount, and they were brought to me. They were no doubt fearful, but stood up straight in defiance of their lot.

The Dacian and the Scythian languages are virtually the same, although dialects vary from tribe to tribe.

I studied the men brought to me in silence, like a butcher deciding which of the sheep to slaughter first. I spoke in unaccented Scythian and said, "All of you have worked in the silver mines in the mountains of Dacia?"

They all nodded in response, only one of them managing to keep his mouth from gaping in surprise due to the Roman speaking fluent Scythian.

"I need you to do one job for me", I said. "It will take a month or three, depending on your level of commitment. When the job is properly done, I will release you to go your own way."

Now all four were gaping.

They were skilled and valuable slaves, and only a fool would let that amount of coin go to waste.

I was no fool. I needed to get rid of witnesses, albeit in a humane way. Releasing them was better than killing them.

In any event, once they had recovered from the initial shock and closed their mouths, I continued. "If you try to escape, my warriors will kill you immediately. What say you?"

They all went down on one knee and one of them spoke. "We will give you our oaths, lord. May we ask your name?"

"I am Eochar of the Roxolani", I said.

All of them had their left foot chalked white, as was the custom, to show that they were imported slaves. I added, "And for the sake of the gods, go and rinse the white chalk from your feet, you look ridiculous."

Two months later they were finished. They had built a timber-lined tunnel from the main dwelling to the dense copse of trees one hundred paces distant. Only the slaves, Cai, Nik and the Roxolani knew about its existence. I swore all of them to secrecy.

Not long after, I set the grinning Dacians free on the Roman side of the river. I had purchased four horses and I gave them ten silver coins each. They were ecstatic.

I tried to ignore my feeling of discontent and enjoy life. I trained with Cai and the Roxolani, spent time with the horses, and enjoyed the company of my father when we supped together most evenings.

But I was losing the battle.

I knew what I wanted to do, but I needed to discuss my ideas with my companions.

My strategy was to speak with them separately. Divide and conquer.

Cai was a reluctant hunter. He would hunt in order to survive, but since we had sheep and cattle on the farm, it was not a necessity.

I persuaded Nik to go hunting with me. Since we would hunt on horseback with our bows, it was not overly taxing for him.

We both took our favourite Hun horse and set off on a near perfect morning. I had my special bow with me, gifted to me by the king of the Huns. Both of us carried a full quiver of thirty arrows.

We were still in sight of the villa when Nik said, "Lucius, Cai and I have been worried about you lately. We have noticed that you are not happy, although you try to hide it."

So much for hiding my emotions. This was one area were my Hun education had failed dismally, I thought as Nik continued.

"I am glad that I can speak with you alone today, son", he said. "It is the perfect opportunity."

I realised that the hunter had become the hunted. Although I felt like a naughty child being lectured, I decided to open up to Nik.

"Nik, you are right ", I sighed. "Although I have all I need and more, my heart is not content. There is something alarming that I have discovered about myself that I want to share with you."

Nik gave me his concerned father look and I continued, "I am only really happy when I am making war. I do not enjoy killing, though, but I enjoy war."

Nik fell silent and stared into the distance. He raised his hand in the manner that signalled danger. I realised that Nik's silence was not due to my revelation, but because he had spotted six men attacking a single rider wearing the uniform of a Roman officer.

We did not hesitate. The bandits were no match for mounted archers armed with the most powerful bows in the Empire.

They did not notice our presence before two bandits lay bleeding in the dust. I had selected hunting arrows with broad, four-bladed heads. The bandits wore no armour and I therefore did not have to waste my needle points.

As Nik's arrow hit the fourth bandit in the chest, the remaining two turned and fled towards the trees. Even though I am a merciful man, I did not wish for outlaws to roam my lands. I turned my horse with my knees while at full gallop to optimise the angle, and in quick succession shot two armour-piercing arrows through the backs of their skulls.

I must confess, in that moment I considered taking the scalps of the bandits, just to see the look on the face of the Roman officer, but wisely abandoned the thought.

I reined in and walked my horse back to where Nik and the Roman officer were waiting.

The young man was not much older than me. His blonde hair and blue eyes told me he was no purebred aristocrat either. Some barbarian blood flowed in his veins.

I decided to break the silence. "Good morning, I am Lucius and this is my father, Nik. We are farmers out on a hunt."

He grinned at me disarmingly. "I am Marcus, a cavalry officer attached to the fourth legion, and you are no farmer, my young friend. I would sooner have believed it had you told me you were Ares."

He grinned again and fell from his horse, unconscious.

Nik and I bandaged the deep cut in his lower leg and quickly had him laid down on a comfortable mattress in our spare room. Cai was a healer without equal and he prepared a potion to administer to our new friend.

Cai was trying to feed him some liquid potion or other when our guest regained consciousness. He seemed to focus on Cai's outlandish features, frowned, and said, "Who the hell are you people?" Then he fainted again.

Marcus regained his strength quickly under Cai's watchful eye. We had tried our best to convince him that we were just farmers, but I doubt that he believed any of it. Marcus's family farmed in the area and he was on his way back to the legion after a few weeks of leave. They had recently fought a hard campaign against the Alemanni tribe in the Agri Decumates in Germania under the leadership of the emperor, Maximinus Thrax. Although the legions emerged victorious, the casualties were heavy. They were encamped near Sirmium in order to enlist new recruits and bring the legion back to full strength.

Marcus insisted to see my bow. He touched it reverently and said, "I have seen Scythian bows, but never something like this. I hope we never have to fight the people who made this. They must fight like the gods themselves."

He eyed me with suspicion. "You saved my life, Lucius, and I don't know why, but I like you. If I had an ala of cavalry that could fight like you do, by the gods, I could make myself Emperor."

I started to protest, but he held up his hand and said, "I know, I know… you are only a humble farmer. Your secret is safe with me."

We sent him on his way three days later. I had made a friend.

Chapter 40 – Decision

Nik poured another cup of the dark red wine. This batch originated in Gaul, an exceptional vintage.

Apart from wine, I enjoyed few luxuries.

I did not covet expensive clothes or golden jewellery. My prized possessions were my Scythian and Hunnic bows, the gladius Nik had taken off one of our attackers, and the jian sword Cai gave me.

I owned a magnificent cuirass of Scythian scale armour made from the hooves of horses, compliments of Bradakos, which matched well with my Hunnic helmet.

My other indulgence was a long-sleeved mail vest I had made to order in Sirmium. It was made from the best quality steel available, with all the links riveted separately, rendering it almost impervious to sword or spear strikes. It had cost me nearly five times the price of a legionary issue mail vest. When it came to armour and arms, I did not mind to pay for quality.

Cai's laminated silk armour was also special to me. I maintained and cleaned it regularly because I realised that it was virtually irreplaceable.

I stood to refill my cup when Nik said, "Lucius. You must do what the gods demand of you, only then will your heart be at peace." I came back to reality from my preoccupied thoughts and spilled most of the wine on my tunic.

Cai continued, "You drawn to destiny Lucius. Accept and embrace it."

I nodded, refilled my cup to the brim, and said, "I will be departing within a week."

I decided to leave my bows and my jian at the villa. There would be too many questions should I arrive with such outlandish weapons. I did pack my fine mail armour and sword, though.

I contemplated joining the cavalry, but the strength of the Roman army lay in the infantry. The purpose of the cavalry was to assist the infantry.

I would join the legion as a lowly infantry recruit.

The Roxolani guards all indicated that they would like to stay on for a couple of years to assist Nik and Cai with the breeding program. My farm was in good hands.

I said my goodbyes to all, and a couple of days later I rode to Sirmium on one of the horses I had recently taken from the bandits. I sold the horse in Sirmium just to get rid of it, leaving behind a very happy farmer. Wearing my old tunic, and with my few possessions in my pack, I walked up to the gates of the legionary camp.

I was nearly twenty summers old and ready to meet my destiny.

Somewhere up above, in the land of the gods, Arash was smiling.

Author's Note

I trust that you have enjoyed the first book in the series.

In many instances written history relating to this period has either been lost in the fog of time or it might never have been recorded. That is especially applicable to most of the tribes which Rome referred to as barbarians. These peoples did not record history by writing it down. They only appear in the written histories of the Greeks, Romans and Chinese, who often regarded them as enemies.

In any event, my aim is to be as historically accurate as possible, but I am sure that I inadvertently miss the target from time to time, in which case I apologise to the purists among my readers.

Kindly take the time to provide a rating and/or a review.

I include the first two chapters of the second book in the series.

The Thrice Named Man, Part II, Legionary, will be available soon.

Chapter 1 – Recruit

"Name?" stated the clerk. I hesitated for a moment because I had been called Eochar for years. Before I could answer, the clerk looked up while tapping his stylus irritatedly on the side of the table, "Are you hard of hearing or just stupid? Name!"

I breathed deeply and replied, "I am Lucius Domitius Aurelianus."

While he wrote down my name he said, "State your trade."

Again I hesitated, but before he could intervene, I replied, "Farmer."

He scowled and said, "That's not on the list, be more specific."

I could read well, even upside down, so I afforded a peek at his list.

"Huntsman", I replied.

He looked up from his writing, making eye contact and willing me to correct the obvious lie, but I kept quiet.

He mumbled "huntsman" while writing it down and continued, "Are you able to read and write?"

I decided to risk a question. "Would that be beneficial, sir?"

Again he eyed me with suspicion and replied, "Yes."

"I am able to read and write, sir."

He wrote, "Claims to be literate, but it is highly unlikely."

The clerk pointed to an area where many new recruits congregated. "Wait there until you are summoned."

I strolled over to the group of at least six hundred recruits. These numbers were a good indication of the heavy losses taken by the Fourth Legion during the recent Alemanni wars.

All the young men were talking and laughing excitedly while standing together in small groups. Everyone knowing at least somebody. I hovered on the fringes, suddenly feeling lonely, and looked around for the opportunity to approach some individual or other in the same predicament.

I spotted another loner, with eyes searching desperately, not unlike myself.

I approached my quarry in a wide arc. I stopped a pace behind him and said too loudly, "I'm Lucius!"

He didn't turn around, but kept his back to me and replied, "Pleased to make your acquaintance, Lucius, my name is Vibius. I hope you are better at fighting than at stalking people." He had me on the back foot, but turned around with a broad smile on his face and clasped my forearm. He continued, "I really am pleased to meet you. It seems that everyone knows everyone, except you and me."

It was time for revenge and I replied, "Yes Vibius, I am."

He looked at me quizzically and I continued, "I am better at fighting than stalking."

Both of us burst out laughing.

Vibius's father worked for the provincial administration somewhere in the East and had recently been transferred to Sirmium. He had not been in the area long enough to make friends.

I told him that my father bred horses nearby, but we had travelled extensively until recently, which explained my lack of friends.

Allow me to digress. I am inclined to speak the truth. Deceit is something I do not enjoy, but I could not share my past and experiences with my friends. Had I told them my truthful story, they would have ostracised me as a teller of tall tales.

I had lived with the Scythians of the Steppes, fought the brutal Goths and commanded seven thousand barbarian cavalry in a pitched battle. Even if they did, would they believe that I am a prince of the Roxolani and that I had been trained as a master of the sword by a priest from the land of Serica? I think not.

Would they believe that my father had murdered an emperor, or that the king of the Huns embraced me like a son? Never.

The only solution was to remain quiet about my past and keep my martial prowess hidden.

Before we could continue our conversation, centurions arrived and herded us into small groups.

We did not realise it then, but the centurions were the lead centurions of the ten cohorts of the legion. Each knew the number of recruits they had to gather to replace the losses of the recent campaign.

It is important to explain the position of centurion in a Roman legion.

He would normally have seen thirty summers or more, and would possess sufficient practical experience gained in battle. A centurion commands a group of ten contubernia. A contubernium being a group of eight men who share a tent and live like a family for all practical purposes.

A centurion is not your friend. He represents the backbone of the legions of Rome. Practical, without mercy, but extremely capable.

Every Roman legion is subdivided into ten cohorts and every cohort consists of six centuries. The cohorts are led by the centurion of the first century in the cohort.

The highest-ranking centurion in the legion would be the centurion in charge of the first century of the first cohort. The

Primus Pilus, or first spear, is only outranked by officers of noble birth.

Vibius and I ended up in the group of the centurion of the third cohort, Hostilius Proculus. In a certain way, he reminded me of Bradakos, my mentor during my sojourn in Scythia.

Hostilius was a brute. Heavily muscled, scarred and devoid of any discernible compassion. Like Bradakos, he always carried a scowl on his face.

In any event, we ended up with Hostilius and that was that.

It was late in the day and we were shown to an area where legionaries had pitched tents for our use. The required tents were erected by each of the cohorts to accommodate its recruits.

The third had not suffered that heavily in comparison with the other cohorts and only four tents were erected to house the thirty-two new recruits.

Vibius and I shared the tent with six young men whose names I fail to recall. We curled up on our felt mats and I fell asleep almost immediately.

The night passed dreamlessly and I woke with a jolt when Centurion Hostilius kicked my leg.

"Wake up dogs, we are going for a little stroll around the countryside."

"Get your arses outside and line up. Leave your belongings in the tent."

A few heartbeats later, thirty-two bedraggled young men stood in line, facing the officer. We wore a mismatch of clothes. Some had beards while others were clean-shaven. Hairstyles varied from close-cropped Roman style to Suebian topknots.

Hostilius allowed his eyes to slowly wash over us. I am sure I even picked up a hint of despair in his countenance as his scowl increased in severity, his knuckles visibly white as he strangled his vine cane.

He used his vine cane to point at the first individual in the line. "First recruit, one step forward, second recruit, one step back. Every second recruit follow!"

Chaos ensued. Eager to please, some stepped back while others stepped forward, leaving confused individuals in the centre, unable to fix the equation.

Hostilius's face matched the colour of his red cloak as he passed between the lines, yanking the recruits into the proper alignment by the scruff of the neck.

Next to the tents lay a heap of shields. They were all damaged in one way or another and probably used for training.

"Fall out, collect a shield, and fall in line exactly as you were", he boomed.

The result was even worse than the first time. While everyone successfully gathered a shield, we were not able to identify where we fitted into the line. We ended up as a milling bunch, arguing about who was next to who.

The vine cane struck my back with such force, I was sure it had broken a bone. "You!" Hostilius yelled, pointing to a spot in the dirt with his cane. I complied.

As soon as he was satisfied that all were in position, he walked to the front of the column. "Follow me", he said as he marched towards the gate of the camp.

We did not march, we walked.

When we reached the gate, which was closed as per regulation, he yelled, "Stop."

Predictably, some of the men walked into the backs of others. Two even fell over.

Although the centurion knew exactly what the situation would be, he was kind enough not to turn around and mete out the required punishment. He just faced forward and waited patiently as the gates were opened.

I had trained with the curved oval roman shield, or scutum, as it was known by the legions and my left arm was used to its weight and feel. I normally trained with double weighted shields, so in comparison the ones we were carrying felt light as a feather.

We had walked only five miles and I could see that most of the other recruits were battling with the weight of the shields. I emulated them, tried to look tired, and allowed my shield arm to sag.

The lengths we go to in order to be part of the collective!

Seven miles out of the camp the centurion called a halt. He had us turn to the side as if to enable him to discuss something with us.

I had trained with horses since before I could walk and I have been taught to scout by the Roxolani and the Huns, who are the best of the best.

I picked up on the approaching cavalry long before any of my fellow recruits noticed anything was amiss.

I was unsure what to do, so I extended my arm in front of my body, but I did not speak.

"What is your problem, soldier? Do you miss your mother?" Hostilius mocked.

"Small group of cavalry approaching from the north, sir", I said and lowered my hand.

He raised his hand, signalling silence and turned his back to us, facing north. Within moments all of us could see the dust kicked up by approaching horsemen.

A group of thirty bore down on us at full gallop. They did not wear Roman uniforms, but were clothed in the style of the Scythians.

Hostilius yelled, "Barbarian cavalry approaching, brace for impact. Keep your shields locked and do not yield!" As he had no shield, he moved behind the shield wall for protection.

I knew what Scythian cavalry looked like. These horsemen were no Scythians. They rode badly, like Romans, and had Roman saddles and horses. Their clothes as well as their weapons and armour looked wrong.

Yet, facing a cavalry charge as infantry is one of the scariest experiences one can have. Then it dawned on me. It was a test.

The cavalry was a hundred paces away when I turned to Vibius and whispered, "These are not barbarians, my friend. The centurion only wants to see who will run. Relax."

At about forty paces out, three of the recruits could not bear it anymore. They dropped their shields and ran. The bogus barbarians reined in and halted ten paces from us.

My eye caught Hostilius watching the recruits intently.

He called to one of the horsemen and said, "Fetch back the boys who ran and bring them to me."

Hostilius stood a couple of paces away, awaiting the return of the cowardly recruits. Everyone was chatting excitedly and patting each other on the back. I focused and tried to listen to the conversation Hostilius was having. The three unfortunates stood in front of him with eyes cast downward.

He spoke softly. "Not everyone is cut out to be a soldier. You three are not. You have not yet received the mark of the legionary and therefore you are free to go home. Do not be disheartened. If this exercise had not been done, your bloated corpses would soon lie on the field of battle."

He turned around, unaware of my eavesdropping, and yelled like only a Roman centurion can.

"Quiet!" he boomed, his vine cane biting into the arms and legs of the recruits nearest to him.

"You may think that you are fortunate compared to those boys", he said and pointed at the three walking down the road. "They are the lucky ones. You ladies now belong to me and I do not suffer fools like you. You will soon curse the day that you were born. Back to camp. On the trot."

I was the only one who did not vomit. I even had to fake looking tired when we arrived back at camp.

Trestle tables had been set out during our absence. One for each of the cohorts, attended by a myriad of clerks.

The twenty-nine of us lined up on the instruction of the centurion.

He stood next to the tables, observing the process.

Two wax tablets were laid out on the table.

"Gaius Cottius", yelled Hostilius. "Approach."

One of the young men stepped forward and came to stand next to the centurion.

"Can you read and write, Cottius?" Hostilius asked.

"Yes, centurion", he replied.

"Read this" Hostilius said, "and then write it word for word on the second tablet."

Cottius smoothly read the inscription and proceeded to copy the text as instructed.

Hostilius handed the writing to a clerk who scrutinized it and nodded in acceptance.

"Congratulations Cottius", Hostilius said. "Welcome to the staff of the quartermaster. Your pay will be double that of a normal legionary."

He pointed with his vine cane to where Cottius should proceed.

"Lucius Domitius Aurelianus."

I saw what happened to Cottius and for the first time in my two-day long military career, I was paralyzed with fear on hearing the centurion call out my name.

If I were to end up in the service of the quartermaster, I would be a clerk for twenty years. I was horrified.

"You said that you are able to read and write. Is that correct or are you a liar, Lucius Domitius?"

"I can read and write centurion", I stammered.

A wax tablet was handed to me. The only thing I could come up with was to read the text, but read it badly, like a child would.

I looked up at Hostilius when I was done reading. His eyes narrowed and he pointed to the second wax tablet and stylus. I wrote, trying to draw the letters badly and change around the letters to confuse the reader.

The clerk checked my work and, scowling, shook his head. My gaze met Hostilius's eyes which were still narrow with suspicion.

He kept his counsel and pointed to the spot I should move to. With relief I noticed that I was standing nowhere near Cottius.

When we had all performed the test, twenty-seven of us were left. A smiling Cottius and another recruit were escorted away to the section that would join the staff of the quartermaster.

It was late afternoon but I could see that the proceedings were long from being concluded.

We were again ordered to line up. We had to wait for a clerk, who arrived accompanied by four legionaries, carrying a heavy chest.

Each of us received our joining bonus of three hundred bronze sesterces. For me it was small change, but for some of the recruits it was more coin than they had ever held in their hands and they were visibly overawed.

I took the coin and tried to look pleased.

Once all of us had received the payment and made our mark to confirm the receipt, Hostilius took over.

"You will now take the legionary oath and receive the mark of the legion", the centurion said.

We all had to face our new comrades and recite the oath, one by one.

"I swear to do as my emperor commands, I swear to never desert my legion and I swear to give my life should it be required."

While we were giving our oaths, our names were entered into the rolls, as the oath would legally bind us to the service.

We then advanced to another table and one by one had the name "Legio IV Italica" tattooed onto the inside of our right wrists, just below the palm.

Once we were done, Hostilius clasped our forearms one at a time and said, "Welcome to the third cohort, legionary. Now you belong to me."

Chapter 2 – Training

"Wake up ladies, time to look pretty for the party." The centurion's voice boomed around the tents.

In the early light of dawn, the cohort barber had set up his mobile station and proceeded to cut our hair short, and shave off our beards.

Barbering thirty men takes time. While we were waiting in line, the centurion shared some of his wisdom.

"Let me give you some advice, boys", he said. "One day you will find yourself fighting for your life against some wild barbarian or other. Barbarians love their long hair and beards. Use it against them. Grab it and pull them closer so they can taste your iron."

"What do you see when you look at my face?" he asked no one in particular. Predictably he received no answer, so he raised his vine cane and pointed at Vibius, standing in line next to me.

Vibius was no fool and said, "Lots of battle scars, sir."

"Good, I see at least one of you has sense", Hostilius replied.

"When you fight, your face tends to get damaged. The surgeon cannot stitch the pieces back together if you have a beard, boy."

About a watch later we were all clean-shaven, with close-cropped hair.

"Now that we've neatened you up, let's go get dressed up pretty. Follow me", he commanded.

Hostilius escorted us to the stores of the quartermaster.

We were issued with the standard military clothing as well as hobnailed boots. We had to make our mark as proof of receipt. The value of the clothing would be deducted from our pay over a period of time.

We tried on the clothing to ensure that it fit properly.

It took forever for all of us to be appropriately attired, and we lined up for inspection before we left the stores of the quartermaster. Hostilius scrutinized us.

He stopped in front of a recruit. "Go get smaller boots, idiot. If you march in those, your feet will be bleeding before we leave camp."

He sent a couple more recruits back to exchange some garment or other, and once he was satisfied that all was in order, we marched back to our tents.

"Take down these tents", he commanded. "You are now part of the elite third cohort. You will pitch your tents in the area set aside for my cohort, but you are still too stupid to be integrated with the veterans. We still need to sweat the stupidity out of you."

He left us to pitch our tents and prepare our evening meal. The veterans were housed in wooden barracks next to where we erected the tents.

The most basic skill a legionary must acquire is the military step. It does sound easy, doesn't it?

For one person it would be easy. To teach twenty-seven recruits to march at a certain pace and maintain formation is much more challenging, especially when most of them are dead on their feet from exhaustion.

We were woken very early the next morning, as usual, and started the day with a five-mile run.

We returned to the camp, prepared our own breakfasts, and then we were back at training.

We marched for the rest of the day, practising our steps. Slow marching. Double step marching. All manners of marching.

We rested briefly during midday, and then it was back to marching again.

This went on for weeks, until we could run and march all day without anyone vomiting.

Centurion Hostilius Proculus did not attend to us every day. Due to his position as lead centurion of the cohort, he had to take care of other responsibilities, but he was the one who directed it all.

Once we could march properly, we were issued a set of lorica hamata, the chain mail armour of the legionaries, as well as a curved rectangular shield, known as a scutum.

We now trained to march in full armour, with shields. Again, it took time to master the little tricks of the trade. Hostilius showed us how to hold the shield in an overhand grip, and where to add extra padding to the undergarment to stop the mail from chafing.

But he was also relentless and brutal. Beating the stragglers mercilessly with his vine cane and meting out punishment for the merest infringement. I am sure that he would have blended in with the Huns. Those thoughts I wisely kept to myself.

All of the recruits were chomping at the bit to get proficient with weapons, but Hostilius refused.

"You will not touch a weapon until you can march perfectly", he said.

Two months into our training we had managed to march the required twenty-four miles within five hours, without breaking ranks or falling out of step.

Although he tried to hide it, I could see our centurion was pleased. Not unlike the feeling you get when your favourite hound eventually manages to retrieve the waterfowl you had downed with your bow.

In any event, nobody tasted his vine cane that day, and on our return we went straight to the training field outside the camp. Fifty wooden posts were erected on one side of the field. The posts were a foot in diameter and stood the height of a man.

We all took wooden training swords from the racks next to the posts as ordered. The wooden swords were exact replicas of the legionary shortsword, or rather, the gladius as we called it.

These wooden training swords were twice as heavy as the real thing because it was weighted with lead.

"Choose a partner, ladies", the centurion said, and pointed to the posts.

We spread out so we all had our own post.

"Show me what you can do", Hostilius said.

Some of the recruits attacked their post with vigour, slashing and stabbing like men gone mad. Others just stood in front of the posts and executed weak stabs and cuts. There were a few who had obviously received basic instruction in the use of the sword and they stepped forward, performed a combination of three or four strokes and stepped back.

I cut at the post with sloppy slashes and for good measure I mixed in a few thrusts as well.

Hostilius called an end to the mess and said, "Lucius Domitius, with me."

I walked towards the centurion and he said, "I am going to attack you with slashes, try to defend."

"Yes, centurion", I replied.

He attacked immediately. I parried the strikes, trying to look clumsy.

We returned to our starting position and without warning he came at me with a perfectly executed thrust to the midriff. My countless hours of training caused my subconscious to take over and I stepped to the right, but at a slight angle, to ensure that the strike would miss my body. At the same time, I allowed his blade to slide along mine. It would allow me to unbalance my opponent and control his blade while I moved in for the killing stroke.

My waking mind realised too late what I had done, but I tried to correct my mistake and I drew his sword onto my midriff. I took the hit on my armour, which was still very painful.

I could see Hostilius's eyes narrow but he willed back his comment and continued, "Do not waste your energy with wild slashing. That is the barbarian way. A well-aimed thrust is much more difficult to parry and will pierce armour, while a slash will not."

"A slash also opens up the attacker's body to counter-attacks, while a thrust does not."

"It is not necessary to bury your gladius in your opponent's body up to the hilt. Give him two inches of the tip, and he is out of the fight."

He proceeded to show us how a technically correct thrust to the midriff is performed. We spent the rest of the afternoon practising this move, with Hostilius making adjustments to our technique.

The centurion left early, with another centurion overseeing the afternoon's training.

We retired early that afternoon as a reward for our faultless marching.

Hostilius left instructions that we be allowed leave of the camp for half a watch to swim in the river.

We went as a group and arrived back at the camp clean and refreshed, albeit a bit tired.

I spent the evening preparing food and talking with my friend Vibius. We enjoyed the basic food and wine rations after the hard training of the day and went to bed early.

We rose before sunrise, prepared porridge, and reported for our morning run, usually led by Centurion Hostilius.

That morning Hostilius was accompanied by another centurion.

"Centurion Tullius will accompany you on the run this morning", he said. "Lucius Domitius, you will stay behind."

I immediately sensed that something was amiss when I heard my name. The tone of his voice was different. It had a nervous edge to it.

The replacement centurion trotted off with the recruits in tow.

I was left standing alone on the parade ground.

"Follow me", Hostilius growled.

We walked out of the camp and stopped next to the weapons training area where we had trained at the posts the previous day.

I was standing at attention and he said, "At ease, legionary."

"I decided to do a bit of investigation yesterday afternoon", he said.

"I went to the office of the procurator and I ended up dealing with a filthy little Greek called Alexander. I enquired about a certain Lucius Domitius Aurelianus, to find out whether his father owns a farm in the area."

"Let me tell you what the Greek told me. To be more specific, he didn't tell me anything, but he had some very good advice for me concerning my health. Do you know what he said?"

It was clear that I was in deep trouble. "No, centurion", I said.

"He told me that the road I am embarking on has just one outcome, and it ends up with my bloated corpse floating facedown in the Danube."

"He also asked me to leave his office and never show my face there again."

"I have been watching you from the start. You knew that cavalry was approaching our group, and you sure as hell knew that it was a ruse. I watched you. You and Vibius were the only ones who didn't look like they were going to shit their breeks."

"I saw the effort you put in to sound stupid when your literacy was tested. Do you take me for a fool? You speak like the patricians do in Rome!"

I could see the anger rising in him, his jaw muscles clenching and unclenching, and his face becoming bloodred.

"Then you try and act like a novice at the posts. You may have fooled your fellow recruits, but I was not born yesterday."

"You run and you don't tire, and you look as hard as steel even though you are still a boy."

"I can see that even now your eyes hold no fear."

I had begun to breathe deeply, to calm myself and to be ready for any sudden move.

His hand went to the hilt of his sword. "I am going to ask you a few questions. Your truthful answers will determine both our destinies."

I nodded and continued to breathe.

"Beware, boy, do not lie to me. I have been a centurion long enough to smell lies a mile away."

"I give you permission to speak freely. Nothing you say will ever be shared with anyone else."

I nodded and said, "Thank you, centurion."

He scowled and said, "Don't thank me too soon."

"Are you a spy for some faction or other of the Roman Senate?"

I looked him squarely in the eyes and said, "No, centurion."

"Are you of the patrician class?"

"Yes, centurion."

"Did you commit a crime and are you hiding from the law?"

"No, centurion."

"Are you able to kill me at will in a sword fight?"

"Yes, centurion."

He visibly relaxed but continued to stare into my eyes, as if trying to find some hidden deceit.

Hostilius walked to the racks containing the equipment and said, "Show me and don't hold back."

He tossed me a wooden gladius of normal weight and attacked.

Within a heartbeat he was lying on his face in the dust.

I extended my hand and helped him up. He accepted.

He walked back to the starting position and attacked me again, albeit using a different strategy.

The outcome was the same.

Hostilius was no fool with the sword, but I had studied under the masters of the sword for years and compared to me, he was a novice.

He eventually shook his head and said, "You truly are a master of the sword. I have never seen your equal. Not in the legions and not in Barbaricum."

"Who taught you?"

"I am honour bound not to answer that question, centurion."

He frowned, the anger visibly rising at my rebuke, but then I saw him calm himself.

"Alright legionary, tell me then, why did you join the legions?"

"To serve the god of war, centurion. It is what makes me content."

He did not answer immediately, but after a while he said, as if to himself, "I, too, am a servant of Mars."

"Where I come from, centurion, we call him Arash."

Printed in Great Britain
by Amazon